THE LAST DANCE

"I want to kiss you," he said.

"What are you waiting for?" she asked, aware that she was weaving back and forth. Wanting, yet afraid to want.

He leaned down and put his mouth to hers. Their bodies pressed in to each other, her soft breasts against his chest. They kissed deeply, as if they'd waited a lifetime for this moment.

Pressing his body urgently against hers, he grasped both her hands in his and held them above her head as he moved in a sensual dance against her.

He kissed her deeper. She pulled against him, her hips rolling and bucking. Suddenly her struggle broke through his frenzied haze, and he realized she was fighting him. Emmanuel immediately released her.

What he saw frightened him. Stark terror shone on her face.

How could he have forgotten that there were secrets beneath her facade?

BOOK YOUR PLACE ON OUR WEBSITE AND MAKE THE ARABESQUE ROMANCE CONNECTION!

We've created a customized website just for our very special Arabesque readers, where you can get the inside scoop on everything that's going on with Arabesque romance novels.

When you come online, you'll have the exciting opportunity to:

- View covers of upcoming books

- Learn about our future publishing schedule (listed by publication month and author)

- Find out when your favorite authors will be visiting a city near you

- Search for and order backlist books

- Check out author bios and background information

- Send e-mail to your favorite authors

- Join us in weekly chats with authors, readers and other guests

- Get writing guidelines

- AND MUCH MORE!

Visit our website at
http://www.arabesquebooks.com

THE LAST DANCE

Candice Poarch

ARABESQUE

BET BOOKS

BET Publications, LLC
http://www.bet.com

ARABESQUE BOOKS are published by

BET Publications, LLC
c/o BET BOOKS
One BET Plaza
1900 W Place NE
Washington, D.C. 20018-1211

All Kensington Titles, Imprints, and Distributed Lines are available at special quantity discounts for bulk purchases for sales promotions, premiums, fund-raising, and educational or institutional use. Special book excerpts or customized printings can also be created to fit specific needs. For details, write or phone the office of the Kensington special sales manager: Kensington Publishing Corp., 850 Third Avenue, New York, NY 10022, attn: Special Sales Department, Phone: 1-800-221-2647.

First Printing: November 2001
10 9 8 7 6 5 4 3 2 1

Printed in the United States of America

ACKNOWLEDGMENTS

I'd like to thank Officer Vincent Givens and Sergeant K.G. Diggs for their invaluable help in researching for this book. Any errors are my own; I always take artistic license.

The wonderful corn pudding recipe belongs to my good friend Virginia Dianne Massenburg. Dianne grew up next door to my aunt in Stony Creek, Virginia. She has been generous enough to let me share her grandmother's wonderful, authentic recipe, and for that I offer my fervent thanks.

Profound thanks for support go to my critique partner, Sandy Rangel, and my husband, John.

ACKNOWLEDGMENTS

Chapter 1

The brother who marched into the crowd ahead of Emmanuel Jones slid his hands into his pockets and glided through a row of tables draped with white linen cloths, pink napkins, china plates, and crystal glasses. Women roared—they clapped. One sister upped the bid to two hundred fifty.

A bachelor auction. Emmanuel observed from a room adjacent to the banquet room while he waited for his turn. Phoenix Dye, the sheriff of Nottoway, Virginia, had *volunteered* Emmanuel and provided a police uniform for him to wear, claiming there were only a few eligible males in the department. When Emmanuel reminded him that plenty of young men were on the force, Phoenix rebutted with, "That's the problem. They're too young. Since you're popular with the women, you'll draw top dollar. The Women's Center needs the money."

Emmanuel tugged at his shirt collar. He was a detective and he hadn't worn a uniform in years.

Brisk footsteps behind him clattered across the wooden floor. Emmanuel turned to see Shari Jarrod hurrying through the little room carrying a stack of papers. Instead of enjoying the brunch like the two hundred women inside, she was busily working. She dressed nothing like her sister, Clarice, who'd moved to Nottoway, Virginia, ten years ago. Shari wore a pair of mud-brown slacks. He couldn't tell if the shapeless jacket that hung on her like a burlap sack hid any curves. The color was all wrong for her honey-brown complexion. It made her look washed-out and drab. Her hair was pulled back into a severe bun befitting a much older woman, even though she couldn't be more than thirty. She certainly wouldn't be bidding, thank goodness. The dates were designed to be fun. "Fun" wasn't in her vocabulary.

Now and then he caught glimpses of Shari grocery shopping or at the movies with her niece and nephew. He never saw her out on the town with other young women her age having fun. She absolutely never crossed the threshold of the local sports bar at the end of the workday, like other Blake Industries employees. The scuttlebutt was she'd still be at the grindstone.

Emmanuel rubbed his chin thoughtfully. The severe hairstyle emphasized rather than detracted from her delicately carved facial features. Only a trace of gloss touched her temptingly curved mouth. There was both delicacy and strength in her face. Of course it would be a challenge to teach her how to have fun. He chuckled and shook his head. He must be out of his mind.

He lounged casually against the doorframe and listened to the DJ from a prominent Richmond radio station woo the women in the audience until the bidding stopped at two-eighty.

"The lucky winner is the lady in purple," the DJ said. The DJ counted down. The bachelor approached the bidder and kissed her on the cheek. The Women's Center representative hustled the bidder to the table to collect information and payment.

Then the DJ announced Emmanuel's name. Smothering a groan, Emmanuel moved forward. It would be embarrassing if he came in under two-eighty, he thought with a touch of male pride, as he marched into the audience. The crowd exploded. His smile widened in approval. He wondered if every woman he'd ever dated was in that assembly. That would be a crowd in itself. Better, would any of them bid on him?

With long purposeful strides, Emmanuel strutted along the front of the stage.

"Ladies, our officer of the peace thinks all women are special," said the DJ.

"Yeah, we know that," someone yelled.

"One hundred dollars," a sister bid.

Keep coming, Emmanuel thought. His reputation—although he was trying to change it—was seriously at stake.

He strolled down the narrow aisles. Women he'd known since pre-school smiled and giggled. He flashed them wide smiles. The bidding climbed. He spotted his sisters, Johanna and Pam, at a huge table with their daughters and a group of friends. He cut over to walk another aisle.

The husbands were baby-sitting the younger children today. "Women's day out" they called it. They were probably at Tylan's place loading the kids up on sugar and greasy fries.

Eighty-nine-year-old Mrs. Drucilla finally raised a lacy handkerchief. "I'll pay a hundred fifty for him."

The crowd howled. "Uh-oh. What's Luke going to say about that?" someone said. "You're already married, Mrs. Drucilla. Leave him for us single women." To the audience's delight, Emmanuel hustled over and kissed Mrs. Drucilla's wrinkled, paper-thin cheek.

Infectious humor set the tone. The bidding increased until it reached three hundred.

That's more like it, Emmanuel thought.

And then he heard "one thousand." Emmanuel froze in a stunned tableau. The crowd grew silent, then the resonance shattered. It took a moment for the DJ to regain control. Once the noise subsided the DJ said, "Do I have a bid for one thousand ten?"

Several heads shook. Nervous laughter tittered. "Who is the lucky woman going on a date with the officer of the peace?"

Then he heard the name. Shari Jarrod, the homeliest, most uptight woman in Nottoway. Call him vain, but if he was forced to participate in the benefit, the least that could happen was for him to get an uninhibited sister to take out on the town. They didn't have to make out, but at least they'd have fun. Shari would be thinking of computer lingo—zero's and one's—over dinner. This was going to be tough. Then Emmanuel got into the spirit of the event. Even he could hang in there for one night.

He scanned the crowd trying to locate her to give her the obligatory acknowledgment, but she must have disappeared into the back room again because he couldn't find her. He joined the other bachelors for a final march, and then they went into the side room. Emmanuel had been there for only a minute when Claudia Rhodes flagged him down and pulled him to a quiet area.

"I need to talk to you, but not here. Can you meet me tomorrow at the park?" She swept her long braids back from her face.

"What's wrong?" he asked. She looked nervous. He knew from as far back as high school, when they'd dated briefly, she always messed with her hair when she was agitated about something. Now, as well as then, she was meticulously dressed. Today she wore a red pantsuit with a black silk tank top. Her lacquered nails were painted an off-white with red decorations.

"I just need to talk to you."

He ran his finger around the tight collar. He wanted to get rid of the uniform as quickly as possible, but he found himself saying, "I'm free now, or we can meet later today."

Claudia shook her head. "Deborah's leaving town tomorrow and I promised her I'd help her pack. I have tomorrow off, though. Meet me at eleven in the park across from the office." She was a nurse in the doctor's office on the corner there.

"Okay."

She gave him a half smile. "Thanks," she said, and touched his arm. Then she turned and walked toward her friend Deborah who'd attended the brunch with her.

Emmanuel wondered why she wanted to talk to him. What was she worried about? He also wished he

could have talked to her right away in hopes that it
would ease her mind.

Anger swamped Shari in waves as she shot into
Clarice Chance's yard, jumped out of the car, and
slammed the door. Her sister had gone too far this
time. Tylan's car was gone. Her sister's husband and
the children were still out. Good, she thought as she
stomped to the door. She and Clarice could hash
this out in private.

Her family was always trying to match her with
someone as if she were only half a person without a
man on her arm. This was the Twenty-First Century.
She was a complete person in and of herself. And
she certainly didn't need her older sister to go out
and beat the bushes to get her dates.

Shari leaned on the doorbell, not noticing the well-
tended lawn and the azaleas that still bloomed laven-
der. Clarice sure was taking her sweet time opening
the door. Shari crossed her arms and tapped her foot
on the marble step as she waited impatiently for her
sister.

A greeting caught in Clarice's throat when she
opened the door and saw Shari.

"How could you?" Shari asked, forcing her way
into the house. "How could you make me the laughingstock of the town by bidding all that money on
that man in my name?" She spat the words out.

Clarice looked taken aback. "We were going to
give the money to the Women's Center anyway. Why
not get some use out of it?"

"Did you stop to consider that if I wanted a bachelor date, I'd bid for my own?"

Clarice scoffed. "Give me a break. You'd never stop work long enough. You're hiding behind work to avoid a real life."

Shari plunked her hands on her hips and leaned toward her sister. "I don't need you choosing a date for me, Clarice, or running my life."

"You won't do it. Somebody has to." Being the oldest sister and the boss of five siblings for many years, Clarice wasn't to be intimidated by the youngest.

"You hated it when Dad butted into your life. Stay out of mine. Now I have to figure out how I'm getting out of the date."

"You can't."

"You bet I can. I'm not going anywhere with Mr. Playboy." Shari threw her hands into the air. "Of all the bachelors, why did you have to choose *him?*"

"Emmanuel is just the one to bring you out of yourself. If you renege, I'm withdrawing my donation."

"You wouldn't. The Women's Center isn't about dates. It's about a sanctuary for troubled women, not about who I will or won't date."

"You think about it. Then you get in the spirit and go on this fun outing. Nobody's asking you to marry him. Just have some fun for a change."

"I'll pay the money."

Clarice crossed her arms. "And get more notice from the paper? I can see the front-page article in the *Review* on you pulling out. How would *that* look for your charity event?"

Shari went from resentment to frustrated anger. "Clarice, I'm not a snot-nosed six-year-old. I'm thirty. I can pick my own dates. I can date if I want to, work the hours I choose, and stay home on Saturday nights if it pleases me. This is my life, not yours. Stay out of my affairs. I'm tired of everyone thinking that just because I'm the youngest, I don't have enough sense to make my own decisions."

Clarice was taken aback. "Shari . . . I never thought that."

"I know. You consider me a baby, like your six-and eight-year-old kids."

Her sister looked stricken. "I'm just concerned."

"You don't need to be." Shari slammed out of the house, anger riding her like an undulating wave.

One night, she thought as she jerked the car door open and climbed into her Mazda. She could put up with Emmanuel Jones for one night. For the Women's Center, she'd do it. But this interference had to stop.

Shari sighed. Even though she loved her job at Blake Industries, she wondered if the loss of freedom in moving into the same town as her older sister and brother was worth the generous pay and benefits.

Then a smidgen of conscience beset her. Perhaps she'd been too tough on her sister. But Clarice was getting as bad as her parents were, trying to set her up with a man. As if a woman couldn't have a life unless a man played an integral role in it. With some of these men as examples, she'd prefer to do without rather than put up with the pain and heartbreak they put women through.

She knew she couldn't throw all men into the same bag. Her sister was blessed with a wonderful husband. Her father was a strong male in her life. So were her brothers, who respected, admired, and loved women.

It was just that she hadn't been blessed with the

kind of relationship her sister had. She didn't envy her. She was happy for her. But that didn't give Clarice the right to interfere in her life. And she certainly wouldn't start with the king of Nottoway bachelors.

Shari understood where the impetus came from. Clarice was the oldest of six siblings. Since their parents worked so hard, responsibility for her younger siblings had often been thrown on her. Now that they were all adults, Clarice found it difficult to cut the strings. But Shari enjoyed her comfortable life and she didn't appreciate Clarice stirring a ripple in it.

She neared the turnoff to her house and spun left into the long path that led there. Underlying all of the emotions that stormed through her like a witch's hurricane was not the anger. Underneath it all lay fear.

The next day Emmanuel had just enough time to drive by Tylan Chance's One Stop Gas and Service Station to pick up lunch before he met Claudia at eleven. He drove down a long deserted stretch of country road. It was mid-June and the trees were bursting with thickly leafed branches. So thick in fact that he could barely see into the dark woods on either side of him.

Once again he wondered what troubled Claudia. What was so important that she couldn't tell him about it over the phone or meet with him yesterday? Emmanuel neared a stop sign.

Suddenly a roar came from the adjacent road. Gears shifted. Tires squealed as speed accelerated. Emmanuel swore and looked down the straight road to see a pair of Mustangs. The tail ends of the flashy green and yellow autos streaked away. Shifting into gear, he tore down the highway, siren blaring, top lights flashing.

Within a minute he pulled up behind two brand-new Mustangs and opened the car door with his SUV still rocking to a halt. He jumped out of the car, shouting before he reached either of the other cars. "Get out of the car!"

Two tall, lanky teens stretched to their full six-four heights with identical grinning expressions. "Hey, Uncle E," Karl said, approaching him alongside his sunshine-yellow Mustang. They weren't relatives by blood but by marriage, all made stronger by the friendship between his sister and their mother. His sister was married to their uncle. The uncle who gave them the Mustangs in the first place.

"What the hell do you think you're doing? Don't you realize you can get killed driving like that? Or kill somebody else?"

Karlton was quiet, but Karl chomped on his gum, flashed another grin, ran his hands along the smooth line of the pristine vehicle, showing every bit of the disregard and arrogance of an eighteen-year-old. "Nobody lives near here. We were just trying her out. Seeing what she could do."

"Smooth," Karlton said with an identical grin, though they looked nothing alike. "Real smooth. You remember, don't you, Uncle E? Aunt Johanna told us how you used to race your Super Sport. Nobody could touch you for speed." He leaned toward Emmanuel, stroking his own chin where peach fuzz had started to sprout, and said in a conspiratorial whisper, "You aren't too old to remember, are you?" Karlton was a crafty son of a gun.

"Cute, real cute," Emmanuel replied in what he hoped was a tone stern enough to whip them into shape. Damn if that boy wasn't a diplomat. Emmanuel had to give credit where it was due, but his mouth tightened into a straight line. He remembered all right—remembered the blood roaring in his ears, adrenaline shooting through his veins. Now he realized how stupid it all was. "Don't try that on me. It was just as dangerous and crazy then as it is now."

"You were so notorious, rumors of your races still circulate," Karl said. He was all playboy charm— reminding Emmanuel of himself at that age.

"That may be, but you're parking yours until your dad gets back."

"Ahh, come on," Karl groaned. "That's another whole week. We got dates tomorrow night."

Emmanuel flashed a grin. "Sold that old minivan yet?" When their mother purchased a new vehicle, she had given them the family car she drove. Although having the back of a minivan at the disposal of teenagers raging with hormones left plenty to worry about. Emmanuel wouldn't mind, except Karlton dated his niece. Emmanuel broke out in a cold sweat at the thought of Karlton handling his niece. Because he knew exactly what he'd done at that age.

Karlton snatched the hat off his head and whacked it against his thigh. "We can't show up in that old thing. Not when we got this." He patted his car as tenderly as he would a woman. The thought of the guy stroking his niece had Emmanuel seeing red.

"You've got two choices. Lose your licenses or park the Mustangs until your dad returns. I'm leaning toward taking your licenses." If their father heard of this, those cars would be returned to their rich uncle before they could blink their eyes or conjure excuses. And they both knew it.

Karlton sighed. "I guess I'll have to get Monica to drive me around."

Emmanuel thrust out a hand and hauled the boy close—so close they were nose to nose. "Not on your life," he muttered. "You remember the rules."

"I'll just follow your sterling example."

Emmanuel's stomach roiled. "You got a death wish?"

"Don't get so bent out of shape. I'm always respectful of her."

Emmanuel let the boy go. The reminder of his notorious past with women wasn't something he was proud of. But he'd changed, or hoped he had. And he didn't want the boy experimenting on his niece. Talking to Monica did no good. She was in love with the fool.

"You'd better not hurt her."

"Don't worry. I'm not leaving behind a string of broken hearts, unlike you."

Emmanuel had never meant to hurt anyone. It was just that the relationships never worked out— something was always missing. But he detested having his past thrown in his face. He hadn't dated for months now. Nobody seemed to notice.

Emmanuel glanced up as another car approached them. It was the third triplet, Kara, driving her red-hot Mustang. Their younger sister, Phyllis, sat in the passenger seat. Kara stopped her car on the opposite side of the road. "Were those boys racing again, Emmanuel?" she asked as she opened the door and hopped out wearing shorts so scanty, they should be outlawed.

"How are you, Miss Kara?" Emmanuel said, and the boys rolled their eyes.

"Just fine, Emmanuel."

Seven-year-old Phyllis hopped out of the car and bounded across the road, an excited smile beaming from her pretty face, her pigtails flapping. "Who won?" she asked.

Kara groaned.

Emmanuel crossed his arms. "Were you in on this?" Emmanuel asked the little girl, adopting a serious expression.

Speechless, her chin dropped to reveal two missing teeth.

" 'Cause if you were, I'm going to have to give you a ticket."

She found her tongue and shook her head so hard, her pigtails loped from side to side. "You can't give me a ticket. I can't drive."

"But you were an instigator."

Her mouth trembled, her eyes watered. "I don't want to go to jail."

"Stop teasing her, Emmanuel." Kara gave him a stern glare, and then patted her sister's head. "He's not taking you to jail, sweetie. He's just teasing you."

Emmanuel tapped her on the nose and narrowed his eyes. "You're okay, but I can't say the same for your brothers."

Alarm flashed across her little face. "You taking them to jail?"

"No. They just have to walk until your daddy returns." He glanced at the boys. "I'll be by to get your keys."

"Ah, Uncle E. Can we just keep this between us?" Karl asked. "No sense in worrying Dad about it."

Emmanuel thought for a moment. "I'll think about it."

The boys got into their cars and drove away sedately. Emmanuel escorted Phyllis to Kara's red-hot car and opened the door for the little girl. She climbed in and he buckled her into her seat belt and closed the door.

Kara narrowed her eyes at him. "I want to talk to you about the bachelor auction, Emmanuel."

Emmanuel leaned against the car. "What about it?"

"I don't like it. Shari's nice. You shouldn't be playing games with her."

"Hey, I only volunteered to help the Women's Center. A good deed, if you recall. You should be thanking me."

"Don't try any of your tricks on her."

"All in the name of charity." Emmanuel pushed away from the car.

"If you hurt her, I'll never forgive you. I don't want her to be the laughingstock of your little office."

"Hey, I'm not that kind of guy."

"We both know you're a player."

"Am not. I've changed."

"Oh, pu-lease," Kara said, snatching open her door and climbing in. "Remember what I said. She's serious—not to be played with."

Why wouldn't anyone believe him? "Shari's a grown woman. She doesn't need a teenager to take up for her." Emmanuel wished he'd never been a part of that auction.

"Put your seat belt on, Kara," he said.

After she drove off, he glanced at his watch as he crossed the road to his car. It was too late to grab a sandwich before meeting with Claudia, so he drove directly toward the park.

* * *

As Emmanuel approached the small park in downtown Nottoway, he didn't see Claudia's mint-green Toyota. He was a detective now, but even though he didn't do traffic, he still knew every car. He drove into an empty space in a small lot, parked, and waited for her to arrive. The day was warm and the humidity climbed high, so he left the motor running for the air conditioner.

When he'd passed two hours earlier, the park had been deserted. Now it was teeming with people. An early lunchtime crowd had gathered, filling the picnic tables and benches under the oak trees. The people carried lunches in brown paper bags or colorful plastic containers. Toddlers played in new sand pits or on swings and new monkey bars that had been installed a month ago.

When he finally exited the police-issue SUV, he heard a high-pitched scream. He stifled an oath as he ran across the clearing to a thick grove of trees next to a huge weeping willow.

Heads turned and people started to move quickly in that direction. As Emmanuel neared, a crowd was already gathering. A couple of women had thrown their hands to their stricken faces and tears ran silently down their cheeks. Men looked on in horror. "Call 9-1-1," someone called out.

"Stand back, please," Emmanuel said, pushing his way through the crowd.

Claudia lay sprawled on the ground, her hands and ankles taped together with white athletic tape. What earthly reason would someone have to kill her? Everyone loved Claudia. But at least one person didn't.

"Oh, my God. The serial killer is here!" someone cried out.

Emmanuel couldn't think coherently for long excruciating seconds.

Then the police detective in him kicked in. He moved forward, stooped, and checked for eye movement and airway breathing then felt for a pulse, which he'd already guessed wouldn't be evident.

She wore a sleeveless blue nightgown, as if someone had dragged her from her bed. He glanced at her bare feet and the lack of evidence of a struggle at the scene. Her skin was cool to the touch. He gazed into her lifeless eyes; they seemed to appeal to his sense of justice to find her murderer—even though it would be far too late to save her.

Her purse lay open beside her, the contents spilling out—including a wallet with cash that had been haphazardly stuffed inside along with the usual jumble of a woman's purse. Why would the murderer trouble to get her purse when she wore a nightgown?

Emmanuel noticed the crowd closing in. "Please stand back so you won't destroy evidence," he said as he took the cell phone from his breast pocket and dialed headquarters. He reported the homicide, asked for the rescue squad and extra personnel to secure the scene.

After the call he stood and perused the crowd. "Did anyone see or hear anything?" he asked.

"Oh, my God!" someone wailed. Several heads swiveled from side to side.

"Not me," a shaky voice rang out.

While he waited, he questioned the group about whom they'd seen before he arrived.

Chapter 2

Emmanuel spent the next several hours in the park gathering evidence. A reporter from the town's only paper had made a nuisance of himself and a helicopter from a Richmond news station had hovered overhead. The coroner had arrived at the scene quickly and now Claudia's body was on its way to the forensics lab in Richmond for an autopsy. Emmanuel had called earlier for an officer to get a judge to issue a search warrant for Claudia's home. Then he'd returned to the station. While he waited for the warrant he donned gloves and went through Claudia's purse. Lipstick, a compact, a wallet with cash, checkbook, and credit cards, a driver's license, discount cards, a couple of pens, and bits of paper with names and notes written on them. The papers were dingy and ragged. They'd been there for a while.

He regarded the names closely. Deborah's name

with an out-of-town phone number was written on one slip of paper. Claudia and Deborah were best friends. There were about ten web addresses—mostly medical home pages, and a few more. Nothing unusual there. It still puzzled Emmanuel why someone would drag Claudia's body from her home and bring her purse. The murder clearly wasn't connected to a robbery. Had it been, the cash and credit cards would have been taken.

Emmanuel tucked the items into a bag he'd already tagged and stashed it with other evidence in the property room. Then he headed to his office.

For the first time, he glanced around the squad room. The "Thousand-Dollar Bachelor" article from the *Nottoway Review* was attached to the bulletin board. Emmanuel pulled it down.

Then he saw that it had been blown up and posted to his door. He sighed and snatched that down, too, then unlocked his door and opened it. Another copy covered his desk. Office pranks again. He put all the articles in the trash, then settled behind his desk, and focused on Claudia's case. She didn't deserve to die like that. Left on the ground like a piece of useless garbage.

Her husband, Howard, had been going out with other women behind her back since the year they married. Could he have decided that he wanted to get rid of his faithful wife once and for all?

Very few murders occurred in Nottoway, and if one did, there was usually a pretty good idea of who'd committed it. Most perps didn't go through this much trouble to cover things up. Claudia's death had shocked the town. Even now, the dispatchers fielded calls left and right about a murderer running loose and what the sheriff was going to do about it. Phoenix Dye, the sheriff, was out of town attending a convention. Tonight, doors that were normally left open were sure to be locked tighter than a drum.

Claudia's name hadn't been released to the media yet because her husband hadn't been notified, but in a town the size of Nottoway, the news had traveled quickly. Emmanuel had visited her parents' home as soon as he could. He'd stayed an hour. Her brothers and sisters already knew via the grapevine.

Emmanuel looked through the data. Claudia was only thirty and had no children. She hadn't had time to live a complete life. In high school she often said she'd always wanted kids. Emmanuel had always thought that she probably didn't have them because of her bad marriage. He wondered why she hadn't divorced Howard a long time ago. Probably because in Nottoway the mind-set about divorce was still old-fashioned. Couples—especially women—believed it was their obligation to make their marriages work. In Claudia's case, it left her with an unfulfilled life. Had it been worth it?

The phone on Emmanuel's desk rang. He picked it up to find his mother calling.

"Emmanuel, your dad went to Petersburg to Lowes. I'm telling you I'm scared to death."

In the background Emmanuel heard, "Save us, Uncle E. She's holding us hostage in the house. In a minute I'm going to kill Trevor." Trevor was his sister Pam's youngest son.

"Mom, let the kids out. They barely have room to move around in your house. It's nice outside."

"Not with a murderer running loose, I'm not. You be careful, you hear?"

Emmanuel switched the phone to his other ear and picked up his pen to jot notes on a pad. Already he was back to his focus on the case. "I will."

"You got any idea who did it?"

"Not yet." He heard a screech in the background. His mom hushed the kids, then managed to keep them quiet for a few seconds.

"Jill told me it was that serial killer who's been offing those women from Richmond to Petersburg. You've got to catch him, Emmanuel."

"We're on it, Mom." Jill and his mom talked on the phone at least twice a day.

"Did you read the paper today?"

Emmanuel tightened his fingers around the pen. "Yeah, Mom. I read it."

"The article where that fast gal paid a thousand dollars for you?"

Emmanuel glanced at the ball of wadded paper in his trash can and sighed. "Yeah, I read it."

"I've got nothing against Clarice—she's a nice young lady. But that sister of hers must be a desperate hussy to spend that much money to get a date. Not that you aren't worth every penny."

"She's not a hussy. Don't say that about her. She's as nice as Clarice. I think Johanna and Clarice engineered that. She wouldn't be caught dead with me."

His mom sniffed. "Uppity, is she? Does she think she's too good for my son just because she runs that computer department at Jonathan's company? Well, I'm going to have a nice long talk with Johanna about setting you up with an uppity hussy. And the more I think about it, I'm going to have a talk with Jonathan, too, about hiring that uppity something for his company. It's bad for company morale."

"Mom, this has nothing to do with Blake Industries. Don't you talk to Johanna, either. I can handle it. You better get back to the kids. Sounds like World War III in there."

"Just my little grand darlings. We're fixing to make some of my famous ice cream. That'll keep them busy and calm them down. They all love Grandma's homemade ice cream."

Emmanuel loved it, too. "I may stop by for some later."

"You do that, baby. We're making plenty."

For once Emmanuel didn't take the time to reprimand her about calling him baby. It never did any good anyway. He hung up and glanced at the wadded paper again. Then he retrieved the phone to dial Shari. He couldn't get this date over with soon enough. Even as he dialed, he decided to go by her office, so he hung up the phone. Everyone knew she worked late. There was a running joke that she kept her nose to the grindstone.

Gardell Gaines stuck his blond head in the door and waved a paper. "We've got the warrant," he said.

Emmanuel snatched his jacket off the chair and headed out to Claudia's place. He and Gardell drove separate vehicles. It was after five. Emmanuel had been on the job since early this morning and the day wasn't half over.

Gardell had returned from northern Virginia a few months ago when an investigating position in Nottoway had opened up. Gardell was a country spirit at heart and had had enough of the city. He'd left Nottoway ten years earlier when his father, who was then the sheriff, had been convicted of trying to murder Clarice Chance. It was discovered that Gardell's dad also murdered Elonza Fortune more than forty years before when he'd been a young officer.

Emmanuel neared Claudia's house. She lived on a side road that had about seven houses. When they got out of their vehicles, he and Gardell first checked doors and windows for signs of a break-in. The front looked secure.

"Back here," Gardell called out.

Emmanuel ran to the back of the house.

Gardell pointed to the doorknob. "The perp entered through the patio door."

The glass had been shattered, leaving a gaping hole. After first dusting for prints, Emmanuel donned gloves and twisted the doorknob. It was unlocked. They entered a spotless kitchen where everything looked undisturbed, and began to investigate.

"Good evening, Ms. Jarrod."

"Hello," Shari called out, glancing up from her papers. Dean, the security guard at Blake Industries checked on Shari several times each evening. He'd made extra checks this evening. He must have heard about Claudia's murder. The incident had made her jumpy, and she was grateful for his vigilance.

"You doing okay?" he asked.

"I'm fine, thank you," Her eyes darted nervously to the darkened corners of the hallway. The guard was a tall, well-built man, his skin a rich dark hue. His well-honed muscles attested to the fact that he spent considerable time in the Blake Industries gym. She should work out there, too, but she never seemed to find the time.

"Mighty nice evening for you to be stuck at work."

"Some of us have to be."

"You got that right." The walkie-talkie buzzed on his hip. "I've got to go. But if you need anything, just buzz us. We'll be here on the spot."

Shari relaxed, warmed by his caring. "Thank you. I will."

He checked the door across the hall to make sure it was locked and sauntered away whistling. His whistling brought her a degree of comfort each evening. He sang in the men's choir at church, and he had a deep, strong bass that just thrilled the congregation.

Shari returned to work on her monthly budget, which wasn't balancing. Accounting was the most dreaded task in management. She was a computer science major, for goodness' sake. She thought she'd be writing programs for the rest of her life, not sitting in endless executive meetings, planning future equipment projections, or writing evaluations. Wishing she could write a program now, she took her calculator and started adding. She was going to whip up a program for this nonsense to balance with the accounting department's program. Sitting through this each month was a waste of valuable time.

The phone rang and she gladly reached for it. Any refuge was welcome. She'd had the devil of a time getting work done today anyway. She sighed and brought the receiver to her ear.

"Hello, Shari." Her sister's voice was tentative.

"Clarice?"

"You're working late again?"

Shari sighed. "As if that's news."

Clarice ignored her snappy remark. "I called to apologize."

Shari caught her hopeful tone over the wire. Guilt

had stabbed her since the argument yesterday. "Accepted," Shari said, glad to clear the air.

"Is it okay if I stop by after Mrs. Drucilla's birthday committee meeting?" Mrs. Drucilla would turn ninety in August. A group of women were planning a big bash for her.

Shari rubbed the bridge of her nose. "Sure. What's up?"

"I have something for you."

"Clarice, I hope you didn't buy another outfit that will take up space in my already-crowded closet." She didn't wear any of the things Clarice bought her.

"I have dinner, too. Cooked your favorite. Spiced chicken."

Shari's stomach growled. She hadn't eaten since noon. "I'll probably be home by eight, but I'll call you before I leave."

"See you soon," Clarice said, and Shari heard her hang up.

Between the phone ringing off the hook and other interruptions, not to mention the dreaded date with Emmanuel, it seemed she wasn't going to get much work done. She couldn't stop worrying about that date long enough to concentrate.

She'd been attracted to Emmanuel since the very first time she met him at the Nottoway Inn. Shari had ordered a takeout dinner. In the parking lot he was trying to start Johanna's car and called Shari over to turn the ignition while he tinkered underneath the hood. She'd known he was an investigator. She'd met him at her sister's house the week before.

His powerful well-muscled body moved with easy grace, and as she watched him, his profile spoke of power and ageless strength. It sent her pulse spinning. But his notorious reputation preceded him. He was a player, not one to take a woman seriously or date the same one for long. Even knowing that, her attraction to him hadn't receded and that heightened the annoyance she felt with herself.

This was her little secret, however. It would remain her secret, she thought as she dug into the figures again.

Some of Claudia's neighbors were early risers, Emmanuel discovered. This tradition of rising early to feed animals and complete other chores before daylight was left over from farming days. Even though the Robinsons no longer farmed, Mr. Robinson still carried the thread of farming in his blood. He couldn't resist keeping a few cows. While he fed his cows each morning, Mrs. Robinson would climb out of bed before the crack of dawn to prepare breakfast. Her kitchen window faced the Rhodes's place. If a strange car drove that narrow road, someone should have seen it, or at least have heard something.

Mrs. Robinson was hanging a wash load on the clothesline when Emmanuel approached. He had gathered fingerprints and other evidence from Claudia's house and was ready to question possible witnesses. The barn stood a couple of hundred yards in back of the clothesline in a fenced-in area where the cows now roamed. Claudia had often complained that the cows got out and chased the kids in the neighborhood. The barn was old and weather-beaten, with a rooster weather vane a salesman had sold to them years ago standing on top. The vane didn't work too well because lightning had struck one corner of the barn a few years back.

"How are you, Emmanuel?" Jillian Robinson called out.

"Pretty good, Mrs. Robinson." Emmanuel started to put his foot up on the cement top covering the well and then he saw a rifle that looked older than him leaning against it. He picked up the gun and checked for bullets. It was loaded.

He glanced at the slight woman who reached into the laundry basket for a towel and snapped out the wrinkles. Her appearance was that of a gentle woman. And she was actually, but fear brought out the protective side of people.

"Mrs. Robinson, you can't leave a gun lying around. Too many kids live around here."

"I've got to have some protection while I'm hanging out my clothes."

Emmanuel unloaded the gun and set it back in place.

A pair of white polyester slacks and a white knit top with bold flowers splashed across it hung snugly on her slim body. The pristine sneakers on her feet looked comfortable compared with the dress shoes that had cramped Emmanuel's toes the last twelve hours. Mrs. Robinson tilted her head up to peer at him from beneath the wide brim of a sombrero as she pinned the towel in place and gave him a stern look.

"Your mama doing okay? I didn't get a chance to talk to her since earlier today." She and his mom were good friends.

"Yes, she's fine. Got the grandkids today."

She chuckled. "Always loves having those younguns around." She reached into the basket again, put her hand on a pair of her underwear, hastily covered them with a washcloth, and straightened up.

"She does that." Even though it was close to seven, the sun shone bright and hot on Emmanuel's head.

"You've heard about Claudia?" Emmanuel asked.

She nodded. "The news liked to knock me down." Mrs. Robinson closed her eyes briefly and shook her head. "God rest her soul. It's a crying shame for something like that to happen to her. I saw you and that other cop over at her place. Find anything?"

"We can't tell yet. We're still going through the evidence." Emmanuel took out his notebook. "Could you tell me when you last saw Claudia?"

Ms. Robinson narrowed her eyes. "I saw her yesterday evening 'round eight. She was coming home from somewhere. She waved to me." A couple of tears slid down her cheeks, and she hastily wiped them away.

"Do you know of any problems she had—any family problems?"

"Other than that no-account husband of hers, I don't know of any. It was always real quiet over there. Of course, he was more likely than not to be gone most of the time."

"Did she change her normal routine?"

She shook her head. "She came and went as always. She and Deborah were always going someplace. She'd see me in the yard and come over now and again to talk. She loved my pineapple cakes. I took some over sometimes." Mrs. Robinson briefly closed her eyes and blew out a long breath. "I'm sure gonna miss her. She was a good girl."

"Did you see any signs of alcohol abuse or increased medical drug use? A change in behavior?"

Mrs. Robinson looked shocked. "No. Never. Like I said, she was a good girl. She'd never do nothing like that."

"Her personality. Had it changed?"

She shook her head again.

"Did she seem upset?"

"Now and then. But that wasn't any different than any other time. I guess her husband's fooling around upset her sometimes. It would any woman. I know I woulda been. I told her a long time ago she shoulda took a skillet upside his head. Straighten him out some. That's what we woulda done in the old days."

"Now, Mrs. Robinson, you can't do that now."

"Why not?"

"It's illegal."

"Some things are personal 'tween a man and wife."

Emmanuel smiled. He could picture her applying a skillet if she thought it were needed. Poor Mr. Robinson. Emmanuel hoped he never got out of line. He'd hate to have to arrest the woman standing before him. She wouldn't come easily. "I was wondering if you've seen any unusual cars out here early this morning, or anytime lately."

She shook her head from side to side. "Just Howard's. He left round five-thirty, his usual time." She put a finger to her lip. "Of course, I thought I heard a car pass just before, when I was getting ready to brush my teeth. Thought he'd already gone. But his car was just pulling out when I got to the kitchen to start breakfast. I must have been mistaken."

"Do you know what time you heard the first car?"

" 'Bout ten minutes before I came to the kitchen."

"And you're sure Howard left at five-thirty?"

"Five-thirty. He always leaves that time."

He snapped his notebook closed and shoved his pen in his breast pocket. "Thanks, Mrs. Robinson."

"I guess I'll get ready to leave for work. I got a night job at Jonathan's company now."

"Good for you."

"You tell your mama hi for me, you hear?"

"Will do." Emmanuel handed her the bullets, warning her again not to leave a loaded gun around. Then he trotted to his car and shucked his jacket, throwing it into the backseat. He turned the air conditioner to full blast and headed out to interview other neighbors.

At a quarter to eight, a knock at Shari's office door startled her. She was so engrossed in her accounting that she jumped as she glanced up to see Emmanuel leaning against the doorjamb, looking lean and handsome.

"Hi there," he said, and sauntered into her office with all the arrogance of a policeman. He wore a navy sports jacket and matching slacks with a striped shirt. He tugged at his neckline.

Shari was annoyed at his impromptu visit, and she was embarrassed about the exorbitant amount her sister paid for him—in her name. His sexual magnetism that seemed a natural extension of him only added to her irritation. Instead of a normal greeting, she found herself snapping, "How did you get in?"

He smiled a slow tired smile. "I'm a detective. If I can't find a way in, who can?"

He was just too full of himself, but she couldn't suppress an inward smile. "I guess it helps when you're the owner's in-law."

He flashed a sexy grin that must be a natural part of him and undoubtedly one of the reasons women clung to him. "That, too," he said, and eased his long frame into the chair facing her desk. She knew that the breadth of his shoulders wasn't the padding alone. She couldn't count the times she'd seen him at her sister's house dressed casually in a T-shirt and shorts.

Shari began to feel very warm. Her large office felt closed-in and cramped. Had the air conditioner suddenly knocked off?

In a nervous gesture, she pulled off her reading glasses and dropped them onto her desk. "How may I help you?" she asked in a crisp tone, leaning back in her chair as if annoyed at his intrusion. She was.

"I came by to set a date with you for the dinner cruise. Is Saturday okay with you?"

Shari glanced at her computer screen and scanned through her schedule even though she already knew she had nothing planned—nothing pressing anyway. "Saturday works for me, but you could have called."

He cleared his throat. "I was in the neighborhood. I'll pick you up at three?"

"Three works for me."

"That'll give us plenty of time to get to Norfolk to board the ship."

Shari nodded.

A squeaky cart announced Mrs. Robinson's arrival. "Hey there, Emmanuel. You didn't tell me you were coming here."

Emmanuel stood. "It was a last-minute decision."

She frowned after Shari as she made a cursory swipe

of the bookcase with her feather duster. "Lord, child, you should go home at a decent time some nights. Dean told me Emmanuel's taking you out. I'm sure glad of that. You need some time off from work." She glanced at Emmanuel. "Every night she's here working late," she said as if Shari wasn't sitting across from them. The woman strolled slowly to the trash can. "You treat her good, you hear? She doesn't get out enough. Not good for a body to just work all the time. I keep telling her she needs to take some time off for fun."

"It's not really—"

"I'll make sure she has a good time, Mrs. Robinson," Emanuel said quickly.

"You do that," she muttered as she gathered up the plastic bag in the trash can. She glanced down at the paper and narrowed her eyes. "What's this here?"

"Trash," Shari said hastily. "Just toss it out." She should have sent the article through the shredder.

The woman pulled the newspaper from the trash can where Shari had tossed that ridiculous article at lunch. Its headline read COMPUTER GURU PAYS A GRAND AT BACHELOR AUCTION. Shari cringed every time she thought about it. Her traitor sister and Emmanuel's too-rich sister scheming together. One would think their husbands and children would keep them busy, but no, they sat back on their behinds guzzling Mimosas and scheming up events for Clarice's nerdy sister.

Mrs. Robinson smiled and winked at Emmanuel. "She paid a lot of money for you, Emmanuel, you rascal. You make sure you're worth it." She chuckled, tore out the article, and smoothed out the crinkled paper. Taking her time, she folded it nicely and tucked it into her pocket before she dumped the trash and left.

Emmanuel looked embarrassed.

Shari wished she could sink through the floor. Emmanuel Jones was the last man she'd choose for a date. By now he must have been through all the single women in Nottoway. How could Clarice possibly think she'd want a player? How could Shari be attracted to such a man?

"Do you want me to walk you to your car?" he asked in the unnatural silence.

"No, thank you. I'll call someone in Security when I'm ready to leave."

"Okay. I'll see you Saturday."

"Yes, Saturday."

He left, and Shari finally relaxed. Glancing at the figures again, she felt the heat that wouldn't recede from her face. Why was she making an issue out of this? It was only one night. She hated the sly looks she'd been getting all day from her employees. They all seemed to be thinking she had to buy herself a man to get a date. The implication was she couldn't get one on her own—as if she wanted one.

With self-righteous indignation, she glanced at the clock and realized the time had flown. Eight o'clock. She was angry all over again at her sister and first thought not to call her. But she called Clarice anyway and asked her to come by later. It would give Shari enough time to cool down. She logged off the server and stuck the accounting sheets back into the folder. Then she called Security.

* * *

Waiting in Howard's yard, Emmanuel munched on a cheeseburger he'd brought from the Riverview Restaurant. The wait gave him an opportunity to think.

Night had finally fallen, clear and crisp even though darkness still hadn't settled in completely. The crescent moon made an appearance. He and Claudia had sat in the car on a night such as this years ago when they'd broken up; they'd both been eighteen. The dissolution of the relationship had been a mutual agreement, but separations were always painful. She'd wanted a serious relationship; he hadn't. She wouldn't settle for anything less. His relationship with Claudia had been the closest he'd come to loving a woman, and even his attraction to her hadn't crossed that barrier of wanting his distance, his own private space. He still wasn't capable of extending himself that far.

Half an hour passed before Howard finally arrived looking tired and bedraggled. He took off his billed cap and rubbed the back of his hand across his forehead.

"How are you, Emmanuel?" he asked as Emmanuel approached him.

"Okay," Emmanuel responded. He fell in step as they moved toward the house. In situations like Claudia's, the department looked at home first, and they'd ask questions such as what the husband would gain by his wife's death. Money from insurance, the dissolution of a marriage? Both situations fit, he thought as he tried to gauge the older man.

"Surprised to see you here. I see Claudia's home,"

Howard said as he opened the side door. "You should have rung the doorbell. You can't see the light from the bedroom."

"Let's go in and have a talk," Emmanuel said.

Howard stepped over the threshold and called Claudia's name.

"She isn't here," Emmanuel told him.

"She must have gone out with Deborah." He chuckled. "They're as thick as thieves."

"Why don't you have a seat?"

"I reckon I will. I put in a long day. What can I do for you?" He acted innocent enough as if he truly thought his wife was coming home tonight.

"I'm afraid I have some bad news." The answering machine flashed a red light. Emmanuel heard a car pull into the yard. He knew he couldn't delay. "Claudia was murdered today."

Howard sat down hard on the kitchen chair. "Murdered, you say?" He looked stunned.

Emmanuel nodded, watching as the man gripped for balance.

"Claudia?"

" 'Fraid so."

He slumped in the chair and shook his head in disbelief. "Oh, my God," he said, staring blankly for a moment, and then he started to cry.

Emmanuel heard the knock at the kitchen door. As Howard sobbed, Emmanuel opened the door to a somber trio—Howard's mother, father and sister.

"Hey, Emmanuel." Howard's mother stepped over the threshold but looked past Emmanuel when she heard her son's sobs. Emmanuel moved aside as the woman rushed to Howard.

"Lord have mercy," she said and gathered him

into her arms. "The Lord is with us even at times like these."

Mr. Rhodes and his daughter came in, nodded toward Emmanuel and followed in Mrs. Rhodes's footsteps.

Emmanuel went outside, closing the door behind him and allowed the family privacy in their bereavement.

He hoped that the tears Howard shed were real. He hoped somewhere in Howard's heart there had been love for Claudia. He hoped that Claudia had carved some happiness for herself in her miserable situation. If Howard *had* killed his wife, Emmanuel would turn every screw to make sure he paid.

Immediately after she arrived home, Shari showered, using her favorite scented shower gel. The warm water cascading down her body felt delightful as it washed away some of the strain of a hot busy day. She spent a half hour there, then stepped out of the claw-footed tub that she loved so much onto a fluffy rug. She toweled off, thinking of Emmanuel's large slender fingers. Pouring cool scented lotion into her hands, she rubbed it all over her skin before donning a baggy tank top and comfortable cotton drawstring pants. Then she ran downstairs and rummaged through her cabinet. Her cupboard was practically bare. A shopping trip was in order. Right now she was glad that Clarice offered to bring dinner, she thought as she waited for her sister to arrive.

Maybe she'd go to bed early tonight. She taught self-defense at the Women's Center tomorrow night. The first class had been last Thursday. Only a few women attended. She hoped more would arrive tomorrow. Two weeks ago, the sheriff had offered to send over an officer for assistance.

Clarice knocked on the door and Shari answered it.

Her sister lugged a garment bag with Paula's Boutique emblazoned on it, along with two shopping bags. She handed one of them to Shari. They moved into the family room and Clarice laid the items on the sofa. Shari put the bag she held on the table and sniffed as the aroma of onions and other scents emerged.

Shari frowned, glancing at Clarice's packages. "I hope that isn't for me."

Clarice nodded and tightened her lips with a determined expression on her cinnamon face. "Yes, it is. It's about time you start dressing in something more appropriate than baggy grandma clothes. Mrs. Drucilla dresses more modern than you do."

"Thank you very much, but you wasted your money," Shari snapped, unwilling to start another argument. She turned her back to Clarice, dug into the bag on the table, and lifted out the Styrofoam plate covered in aluminum foil.

"You can eat later," Clarice said, tugging the dress out of the garment bag.

"I can eat now. . . ." she began and stopped. The green silk dress spilling into a flowing line was the most gorgeous, sexy dress Shari had seen in a very long time.

"I went by Paula's," Clarice continued. "This just came in and it had your name written all over it. I've got the matching shoes, too."

The excitement on Clarice's face brought another

smidgen of guilt to Shari, but she couldn't accept. "Clarice, please take that dress back. It's too ... revealing. It's not me."

"Oh, please," Clarice muttered. "It's time you started dressing your age. I don't know what's come over you. Has something happened that I don't know about?"

Clarice's train of thought alarmed Shari. "Of course not. It's just that I like to buy my own clothes. Wear what I'm comfortable with."

Clarice smoothed the dress over the chair. "Come on, try it on."

Shari turned stubborn. "I'm not wearing that dress."

Clarice planted her hands on her hips. "I want to know what's going on. You used to dress attractively. Short dresses, shorts in the summertime instead of long, hot slacks. It's eighty-five degrees outside for crissakes." Clarice was getting too suspicious. If Shari made a case of it, her older sister would keep prying.

"Okay, okay. I'll try it on."

Clarice narrowed her eyes. "Right now. I want to see you in it—now."

"I'm not one of your children," Shari replied. Nevertheless, she took the dress and shoes and escaped to her room, resentful that she was pushed into trying on a dress that she wouldn't wear. She wrenched off her clothing and slid the silk over her head. After work tomorrow she'd planned to shop for a basic black dress to set off with select pieces of jewelry. She smoothed the lines of the dress and glanced at herself in the mirror.

She looked ... sexy.

She wouldn't wear this dress in a million years. The

V ended between her breasts. In back it dipped so low that half her back was exposed. Stepping out in a dress like this was begging for trouble that she couldn't handle. Then she stopped herself. *It's not the clothing that you wear.*

Clarice stood in the doorway, a knowing smile spread across her face. "That is so lovely on you." Clarice went to the bed and retrieved the green shoes from the shopping bag. "Try these on."

Resigned to humoring her sister to get her out of the house, Shari took the shoes and slid her feet into them. They fit like a glove.

"With my pearls, the outfit will be perfect." Clarice extended a thin box in her hand. When Shari ignored it, she placed the box on the dresser and retrieved the beautiful pearls Clarice's husband had given her on their first Christmas together.

"I'm drawing the line here. I can't wear your pearls."

"Tylan won't mind. You know he wouldn't."

"I can't accept this. They're special. Made just for you."

"You're special, too."

Shari reluctantly measured herself up in the mirror again. A strand of pearls *would* look lovely with the dress. "If I decide to wear pearls, I'll buy a strand."

Clarice shook her head. "I don't know what's come over you, but I expect you to wear that dress on your date with Emmanuel."

Shari frowned at the plunging neckline. "It's too revealing."

"Strut your stuff, girl."

Shari pushed the dress off her shoulders, letting it slide down her body. She stepped out of it, hung it on the hanger, and searched for the price tag. It was suspiciously missing. She handed the garment back to Clarice. While she slipped out of the shoes, Clarice hung the dress in her closet.

"At least let me pay you for it. How much was it?"

"It's a gift."

"I can pay for my own clothes."

"I can buy my sister a gift if I want to. Stop being difficult," she said as she sat on the bed. "What's come over you?"

"Nothing. I don't want you wasting money on me."

"Believe me, Emmanuel won't feel it's a waste when he sees you in this knockout dress."

Shari rolled her eyes toward the ceiling. "My sister's setting me up with a playboy. I still have a bone to pick with you about that."

"A fine-looking, *good* man is what he is. At least you don't have to stop work to shop. Do you know when you're taking the cruise?"

"Saturday."

"Great! And I want to know every detail on Sunday."

"It's just an outing with an acquaintance."

"Oh, come on. Even you can't be that dull. He's about the most handsome bachelor left in Nottoway."

Shari scoffed. "And doesn't he know it! He's dated just about every single female in town."

"You're exaggerating. Besides, he hasn't dated anyone in the last year. He's looking for someone special—someone he can settle down with."

Shari raised her eyebrows. "Those are Johanna's wishes, not what Emmanuel wants."

"Don't discount him."

"Since when did you become Matchmaker of the Year?"

Clarice sat on the side of Shari's bed. "Since you keep your nose in computer programs too much to take care of it yourself."

Shari sighed. "That's the problem. With management responsibilities, I don't have *enough* time to work on my computer."

"With the hours you keep?"

"I'm beginning to delegate more. Kara will be a big help to me, getting some of the routine paperwork in order. The little nuisance things."

"Well, good. The charity auction you planned for the Women's Center went very well. They raised more money than they'd anticipated."

"I'm glad of that. But it's Jonathan and your husband who are really helping it survive. Jonathan's sponsoring a part-time psychologist, and Tylan's help with the office is more than we had hoped for. I'm really grateful."

"Well, the town's grateful that you came up with this idea. Women are using it already. It was needed."

Shari nodded.

"I hope now that the center is a success, you'll take more time for a social life."

"I do other things outside of work. Don't I take time out for your kids?"

Clarice scoffed. "But not for a social life."

"Go home and mother your kids, will you? I'm not baby sister anymore. I'm grown." Shari pulled Clarice from her bedroom and they started down the stairs. Her stomach growled. She had to get Clarice out of the house so she could eat.

Clarice brushed the hair from her forehead. "You'll always be baby sister to me."

Shari groaned. "I'm not going to let you treat me like one."

"I'll come over Saturday and help you out."

Shari scoffed. "I can dress myself."

"I'm taking lots of pictures. See you Saturday." Clarice hugged her and left.

Shari shook her head and watched the car back out of the drive. She rented the house that Clarice had purchased when she first moved to Nottoway. Shari was considering purchasing it if Clarice and her husband would sell. She liked the old house. Since she was single, the two-bedroom structure with a den, living room, as well as combined family, kitchen and dining area was the perfect size for her, as it had been for Clarice.

Shari put a CD on the stereo. Soft music floated in the air as she tugged out the container of food Clarice had brought her. Spiced chicken with rice and greens. As she sat down to her meal, she thought of Emmanuel and how smooth and good he'd looked in her office. She was determined that he wouldn't wear on her. Men like him would never be patient with women like her. They were accustomed to getting what they wanted right away. They wouldn't take the time for some inhibited sister when too many willing ones were waiting on the sidelines.

Chapter 3

Shari moaned. Through a haze, she gazed at herself in the mirror above the bed and the man lying on her, moving urgently against her. She could barely feel his movement, scarcely smell his scent, only just distinguish his slender back in the flickering candlelight. The flickering white lights around the room seemed to merge. She tried to lift her arms but they felt leaden. She attempted to call out to him, but could only move her lips. A sheen of perspiration gathered on her skin as she fought unconsciousness, but whatever he'd given her was stronger than her will. She felt . . .

Shari screamed and bolted upright. Muted light filtered into the room. Seconds passed before she realized that the light actually peeked around the window curtains, not from candles, and that she lay in her own bed. In her own home. Alone. With a shaking hand she pushed the covers back and turned on the bedside light. She wiped the sweat from her face and tapped the remote to her CD player. Soft music drifted gently around her.

Shari pulled the damp nightgown over her head and dropped it on the floor. Cool air raised goose bumps on her skin. She plumped the pillows and sat against the headboard, covering herself with the quilt. She took her teddy bear and held it against her chest, closing her arm around the softness. Focusing on the soft music piping in, she began to breathe evenly. In, out. In, out . . .

She was in her own room, looking at her cherry dresser with its tiny round mirror secured to the wall. Her own personal items were on top. A lace doily crocheted by her grandmother. A Chinese vase her brother Gerald had given her was filled with dried flowers. An antique silver brush-and-comb set Clarice had given her last Christmas. And she sat on her own cherry four-poster bed where the mattress was firm, not so soft that she sank into the cushions.

Her heart still beat far too fast. But now that she'd acknowledged her whereabouts, she closed her eyes and concentrated on only the music. Soon she was humming as the vocalist sang. Before long she began to sing the words.

It had been months since she'd had the dream. At first, the night had seemed so unreal that she'd had trouble recalling anything at all. Simon Reed had slipped the Rohypnol into her drink when she went to the ladies' room. It had occurred two and a half years ago. After a year of visiting a psychologist to help her deal with the rape, she thought she'd put all that behind her.

Half an hour had passed and Shari got off her bed to dress for the day. While she brushed her teeth she tried to analyze the reason the dream had returned. Had the upcoming date with Emmanuel prompted it? Of course not. Despite this little setback, she was over that incident, Shari assured herself as she rinsed out her mouth. After all, she could remember so very little of what had occurred. The illusion of the dream was all she could ever recall. It was the sense of helplessness that had terrified her most and that she found most difficult about her recovery process.

This morning could be considered a classic bad hair day. Shari still felt out of sorts as she started to sip her third cup of coffee at her desk, and she had a feeling this was one of those days that would linger forever. It was a good day to delegate the budget she'd fought with last night, she thought as she picked up the phone and beeped Kara's number.

Kara entered, wearing a short gray skirt with a sleeveless pastel pink blouse, and clunky, thick-heeled sandals. The outfit looked very nice on her. Kara reminded her of herself at that age. Just budding with freedom and an unrestrained thirst for life.

"Yes?" Kara asked in the bubbly manner of an eighteen-year-old.

"I want you to balance Accounting's figures with mine. I've started on it, but I have back-to-back meetings today. Unless you're working on something for Walter." Walter Lamar was Shari's assistant.

"Nothing that can't wait." Kara approached her desk and took the folder Shari handed her. She'd balanced figures before so she knew what to do. As she left the office she hovered by the door.

"Is there a problem?" Shari asked.

"Well, there is something I wanted to talk to you about."

Shari waved a hand toward her chair. Kara closed the door and took a seat with a tentative expression on her face that surprised Shari. Kara was very outspoken, and Shari guessed the young woman needed that trait to survive in a household with two brothers and the sheriff as a father.

She smoothed the folder on her lap and glanced up at Shari. "It's about Emmanuel."

Shari sighed. "What about him?

"He's a nice guy—a great cop. But . . ."

"Yes . . . ?" The girl's hesitancy was beginning to worry her. Shari leaned forward.

"He's a player."

Shari chuckled as she relaxed and leaned against her seat. "Well, that isn't news."

"I know, but . . ." She looked closely at Shari. "What do you plan to wear?"

Shari thought of the green dress hanging in her closet. She wasn't wearing that. "I don't know. Why?"

"I could help you pick out something—at Paula's."

"I know about Paula's. I shop there sometimes." Did everyone—even an eighteen-year-old—think she needed rescuing from her wardrobe? "I think I have something suitable to wear," she said, a little peeved.

Kara nodded. "You're not going to wear one of those . . . those church dresses, are you? The whole town's got its eye on you."

"I haven't decided yet." Shari didn't like the idea of the younger woman getting in her business, but Kara was the owner's niece and a neighbor, so she was giving her more liberty than she would any other eighteen-year-old.

"Like I said, Emmanuel's a player. It would be nice to knock him off his feet—to let him know he's not doing you a favor." She waved a hand in the expressive way teens do. "He's expecting you to look drab, but if you wear something slinky, nobody could think of you as having to buy yourself a man like the paper hinted. Not that I believe a word of that article," she said quickly. "I think it was nasty, and I told the editor so. Any man would be honored to have you. But Emmanuel sure doesn't think he's just any man. He thinks what most of the women in Nottoway do. He's a step above. Show him that you're a step above, too. Let him know he's dealing with an equal or something better."

Shari almost snarled at the mention of that article. Since when did a Jarrod have to buy herself a man? She was good enough for any man—including Mister-High-and-Mighty Emmanuel Jones. "I'll take your suggestion under advisement."

"I'll be happy to shop with you."

Shari glanced at her outfit. She must have given everyone one bad impression of herself. "I think I have something appropriate." She didn't want to wear that green dress, but it did show her figure in a good light. But still . . .

Kara inhaled sharply. "Okay," she uttered, as if to say she'd done her best—and failed.

"And thanks," Shari said as Kara rose from her seat. Shari respected her for caring and having the fortitude to come forward.

"Sure."

Kara sashayed to the door and opened it with all the bravado and self-assuredness of youth. Shari would give anything to feel that safe, that sure of herself again. Once again she wondered if she'd ever get over the rape that ultimately led to her decision to move from Baltimore to Nottoway. True, Jonathan offered her a plum of a deal, but the past had been the catalyst.

Shari lifted her chin and dwelled on the positive. As a result of her counseling, she'd learned and accepted that all men weren't like Simon, and that she couldn't let what happened destroy her life. She had dealt with the downfall. Now she was okay. She was leading a productive life again, she thought as she locked her desk drawer, straightened her serviceable navy suit with its loose-fitting jacket and matching shapeless slacks, and prepared to go to the conference room for her first meeting of the day. The outing with Emmanuel would prove that she was ready to leap over another hurdle. She wasn't ready yet to call it a date.

Emmanuel rapped on Phoenix Dye's door and then opened it. The sheriff wore a perpetual frown that had formed the first day of the triplets' senior year, and hadn't left since. Emmanuel thought he saw a couple of extra lines on his forehead. Because of the murder, he'd come home a day early from the conference. It wasn't that people didn't get killed in Nottoway. It was that you always knew the husband or wife or enemy who did it. Immediately. It was a no-brainer. Or it might be something connected with drugs that was harder to solve, but usually pretty clear.

Claudia's murder was different. She wasn't involved in anything unsavory.

"You sent for me?" Emmanuel asked.

"We have to call a town meeting. The phones are ringing off the hook. Even the mayor's breathing down my neck—and his pest of a wife."

"When and where are you holding it?"

"In the rec center's gym. Tonight—around eight. They have enough bleachers to handle the crowd—I hope."

"Sounds good to me. The whole town's panicking."

"You ever calm your mother down?"

"It was late before I could get over there. Had to spend the night. Jonathan had left work early to rescue the kids. We're going to finish that basement of hers so they'll have someplace to run wild."

Phoenix chuckled. "Who has them today?"

"Johanna. They're terrorizing the tourists in the hotel. Mom went with them to supervise."

Phoenix shook his head, remembering when Mrs. Jones kept his children. "Johanna's brave, letting your mom near the tourists. By the time she finishes regaling them with her take on this latest murder, they'll pack their bags for a safer place."

"Can't find anyplace much safer than here. By the way, the state medical examiner's backed up. The autopsy's been delayed. It won't be done for another couple of days."

"That's another thing. Claudia's family's demanding the body."

"We'll release the body as soon as the autopsy's complete." Emmanuel plucked a string at his buttonhole. "There's something else that I wanted to speak to you about."

"What is it?"

"I was on my way to see Claudia when her body was discovered."

"Why?"

"Sunday, she asked me to meet her at the park."

"Why didn't she want to say what she had to say immediately?"

"I tried to get her to talk to me, but she wouldn't. She said it had to wait. I've been wondering if whatever she needed to tell me has to do with her murder."

"Just for the record, where were you before it occurred?"

Emmanuel smiled. "With the triplets."

Phoenix narrowed his eyes. "The triplets? What for?"

"Kara was dressing me down about treating Shari right. I told her to talk to you if she was concerned."

Phoenix ran his tongue over his teeth. "And the boys?"

"What about them?"

Phoenix shook his head in disgust and reached for a Tums. "I don't even want to know," he said. "I trust you handled it?"

Emmanuel smiled.

"One day you're gonna get yours."

"They're good boys, just feeling their youth."

Phoenix frowned. The last year had been a strain. "I didn't have that luxury at that age."

"You didn't have a sheriff for a father and a rich uncle to give you a brand-new Mustang."

"I've regretted the Mustangs since the day Jonathan gave those cars to them."

"What could you do? Jonathan promised that if they made honor roll the entire year, they'd get cars.

At least you didn't have to worry about homework and skipping school."

Phoenix shrugged. "There is that."

"Of course Victor paid to get their cars suped up."

"He what?" Victor had married Karina when she was unable to find Phoenix after a summer romance. Phoenix had been assigned to an undercover case within the FBI. Karina had been pregnant with the triplets. It was years later, after Karina and Victor had divorced, that Phoenix discovered the triplets were his.

Now it was Emmanuel's turn to groan. "Uh-oh. I thought you knew."

"Hell, no," Phoenix thundered.

"I should have kept my mouth shut. While you're cussing him out, remember that he loves them, too." Phoenix tried to remember that Victor, a really irresponsible man, raised the triplets for seven years before Phoenix even knew they existed. Phoenix still resented that fact—and the fact that Victor still considered himself a part of the children's lives.

"Are they taking the cars to college in the fall?"

Phoenix tamped down his hostility and shook his head. "They're enough of a worry with them here. On a more favorable note, I heard you were the man of the hour at the Women's Brunch. Told you you'd bring in money for the center. Even I hadn't counted on a grand."

Emmanuel groaned. "Don't start. I've been the joke of the department since that brunch. I'm never doing it again."

"Too late. The only thing that will get you out of it next year is marriage."

"Or a convention. I'm going to start working on that right away."

"Not before you solve this case."

Emmanuel left the room. Truth be told, he had mixed feelings about the cruise. He kept thinking about the woman beneath the baggy clothing. Although she wasn't the type he'd usually seek out, something about her intrigued him. Perhaps it was an embedded male reaction that challenged him to bring out the womanly softness beneath. To help her explore her hidden sensual secrets.

Get a grip, he thought as he headed to his office. If her actions last night were any indication, she wasn't going to let him close enough to do anything.

After work Shari arrived at the old school that had been turned into a community center ten years ago. Her sister Clarice had fought tooth and nail for that center when she arrived in Nottoway. Clarice's husband, Tylan, had been her staunchest rival. But Clarice's will had proven stronger than her husband's opposition. Before long he worked with her to make it a success. Now a segment of the community center was designated to the Women's Center, which Phoenix supported.

Shari bolted out of the car carrying a gym bag and ran directly to the women's locker room. She hadn't left work in time to change clothes before she made the mad dash to the center. Quickly she changed out of her business suit into comfortable pants. She then gathered her bags and dashed out of the room, hoping to arrive at class early enough to introduce herself to the officer the sheriff had agreed to send for tonight's class. The officer would give the department's perspective on safety for women and pose as a demonstration sparring partner. By the time she made it to the room where the padding had already been spread on the floor, she was winded and the officer had yet to arrive.

Only a few women had attended class last week—most of them were connected to her sister. Clarice, Karina, Johanna, Kara, Towanna, Pamela and her daughters. If more women didn't join tonight, she wouldn't force the others to attend out of loyalty to her unless they truly wanted the training. Since Kara and Monica were leaving for college in the fall, they really needed to attend the classes. At the last session the girls had promised to bring a few of their friends.

"I guess I'm at the right place."

Shari faced the door and stood speechless. Emmanuel wore a navy chest-hugging T-shirt with matching police-issue shorts. The muscles in his powerful thighs tugged against the shorts. His dress shirts didn't display the gorgeous chest the T-shirt failed to hide. Muscles rippled and flexed as he dropped his bag on a chair. Suddenly he glanced up and caught her staring at him. He lifted an eyebrow.

Shari pursed her lips and remembered that he'd spoken. "Yes, since I'm here, you must be."

Emmanuel smiled, but didn't respond. Shari was acting churlish. He hadn't done anything to warrant her snappy response—except be here, and that wasn't a crime. After all, she'd asked for someone—not him personally, but for an officer. So who was she to complain?

Shari cleared her throat. "Thanks for coming," she finally said. "And please excuse my unkind remark."

"Think nothing of it. I expect your class will be full tonight."

"Why?"

"The murder. Everyone and their mother will want to know how to protect themselves."

"I hope they will take it seriously and want to continue the class to the end."

He shrugged those broad shoulders. "We'll see."

Two women entered the room dressed in black spandex shorts and skimpy matching tops. Soon six more women arrived—and none of them had attended last week's class.

Emmanuel shook his head. Even on a hot summer day, Shari still wore long, hot stretch pants. He wondered at that and the fact that she'd pushed so hard for the Women's Center. Had something happened in her past that made her a proponent for protection? Had she been mugged, or had her home been broken into? Or God forbid, had she been raped?

He watched her closely. She was a no-nonsense kind of woman—extremely uptight. But he wasn't given long to dwell on her. Someone tugged at his arm and he glanced to his left.

"Hey, Emmanuel."

He shifted his sights to the woman who'd spoken and stifled a sigh. "Hi, Kelly."

She sidled over to him. "You had that date with Teach yet?"

He shook his head.

She looked him over like a piece of steak she was selecting in the supermarket. "I sure wish I could have gotten that bid. I bid on you, you know. Up to two hundred. I couldn't afford a thousand. Some folks got money. Some of us have to work hard for the little that we earn." She smiled. "Maybe you could make it up to me by inviting me out. I'm one of the best cooks in town." She lowered her voice to an even more seductive level and ran her long fingers along his arm. The lacquered nails snagged at him.

Emmanuel tensed and removed her claws. "I'm sure you are."

"And," she whispered, "I know how to please a man. You'll never leave my place wanting . . . for anything your heart desires." She tapped him on his chest as she tried to score.

Emmanuel caught her fingers before the nails scored. A few months ago he'd vowed to himself that he was through with meaningless affairs. And her approach certainly wasn't a turn-on. "I wish I had the time, Kelly," he said, "but this murder has me working day and night."

"I'm available—at your command. You could come by anytime—anytime at all." She lost the smile. "I'll be waiting for you."

"That's real sweet of you, Kelly." He heard Shari's long disgusted sigh just before she glanced at her watch. "But no thanks."

Clarice and Johanna rushed in the door followed by Kara and four of her friends.

Shari asked everyone to get into place, and not a second too soon, Emmanuel thought as Kelly slithered back to her place a few feet from him. For some reason, Shari's freshness appealed to him much more than Kelly's brazen attempt. He wasn't about to start anything with the uptight woman, but something about her tugged at his strings. Even the bun she wore behind her head began to appeal to him. The more he saw it, the more he wanted to take the pins

. . . *Stop it,* Emmanuel told himself. With her hair pulled back, her lovely facial features stood out, but he'd love to see her hair loose about her face. The way she tried to hide her charms behind the clothes, he guessed she didn't realize or care how attractive she was. *That's* what had eluded him before. She wore unattractive clothing as a shield.

Puzzles always intrigued Emmanuel. And Shari Jarrod was a puzzle he'd like to solve.

He glanced around the room. He'd been right. More than thirty women of various ages milled about, dressed in shorts—not long pants like Shari. She walked to the center of the room.

"Good evening," she said. The class greeted her in response.

"I think you all know Detective Emmanuel Jones."

"We know him. Hey, Emmanuel." A couple of women in the far side of the room waved to him.

"Good evening," Emmanuel said. "It's good to see so many of you here tonight."

"We're delighted to see you," Kelly said to a few giggles in back of the room.

"Why don't we sit on the mat?" Shari said. "I'm going to begin class by talking about protecting yourselves—about how *not* to be a victim." Shari watched as everyone lowered themselves on the mat—some more easily than others. She also watched the woman Emmanuel called Kelly who sat as close to where Emmanuel was standing as she could. Kelly was scantily dressed—more so than anyone else. She had no hang-ups about her.

"Have any of you heard of the drug Rohypnol?" A few hands waved in the air. "Rohypnol is sometimes called Roofies. Another drug called GHB or gamma hydroxybutyrate has a similar effect. Sometimes it's referred to as Gamma-Oh or Liquid Ecstasy. Although we will learn physical self-defense techniques in this class, we also must be mentally aware of our surroundings, what we do when we're among other people and find ourselves in trouble. Our focus is on how to prevent yourself from becoming a victim."

Shari moved along the front of the room while she talked. "How many college students are here or how many of you plan to attend this fall?" Several hands rose in the air.

"Let's say you decide to go out with a date. He takes you to a club. You order drinks. You make a pit stop at the rest room, but you've only finished half your drink. Money is tight. You return to your table and continue drinking. In a few minutes you begin to feel woozy. He offers to take you home. But instead of taking you to your home, he takes you to his place or drives off to some secluded area. Now you're alone, you're unprotected, and you're quickly losing consciousness."

Shari looked at the faces surrounding her. "Once you felt the effects of the drug, where did you go wrong?"

Kara raised her hand. "You shouldn't drink from a glass once you take your eyes off it or if you leave the table."

"That's correct. And once you start to feel dizzy, you should ask for help from someone you know at the club. Under the effects of these drugs, you have a ten- to twelve-minute window before you lose consciousness. The best scenario is to go with a friend whom you can trust. Check on each other throughout the evening. If you feel something is wrong, leave only with that friend. Never leave with someone you just met."

"Isn't that being a little paranoid?"

"It's called being safe. Better to be paranoid than a victim." Shari talked on for three more minutes, then she turned the session over to Emmanuel, to start the physical training.

Shari sat on the mat and listened to his deep voice as he talked. She was teaching these women not to be victims, yet she played the role of victim herself, even after two and a half years. A perfectly handsome man stood up front with her and she was too afraid to enjoy the sight of him. Soon she would go out with him. Would she be too intimidated to enjoy a simple meal—a boat ride? She could use this outing as an opportunity to have a new beginning, or she could continue being the victim that she was. And if she continued to play the role of victim, what was she doing teaching a class of thirty women? When would she feel safe again? Small steps, her therapist had said two years ago when she started a women's group at work that first consisted of the women who had been raped by Simon after he slipped them the Rohypnol. Shari had held the meetings at her house. Several women who had been raped by Simon attended. Surprisingly, other victimized women, whether from spousal abuse or rape, had also attended the class. It was then that she realized how many women suffered in silence. Sure, she'd read articles in the paper or seen reports in magazines and television, but circumstances were different when it hit home.

When Shari had arrived at Nottoway a year ago, she saw the absence of a Women's Center and realized that perhaps it was her place to help start one. Women needed a safe haven—needed someone to talk to when things out of their control happened. They weren't always comfortable going to family. Shari wasn't. Oh, she knew her family would be there for her, but she was the baby. Someone was always trying to take care of her. She wanted to handle her own problems, stand on her own two feet. She was also afraid of the reaction of her brothers. What if they tried to take matters into their own hands and got hurt or killed? She didn't want her family worrying about her—the *baby*. And through that class she realized that she wasn't the only one who felt that way.

She was lucky. If she needed family, they were there for her. But not all women had family to go to.

Shari glanced sideways at Emmanuel. His deep voice was rich and mellow, his movements smooth as he rested his arm on his knee. Perhaps small steps, one at a time, would get her the results she desired. She couldn't run away from life forever. She wanted to live again. She wanted to be the free spirit that she was before the rape. And she realized only *she* could get herself there. She'd had the counseling. She was enjoying her life again—though not fully. She still hadn't ventured out on dates after her very first attempt.

The class was over and so was the town meeting. Since Shari and Emmanuel hadn't had time to store the mats before the meeting, Emmanuel helped her store them afterward.

He stacked one mat in place in the closet. "I'm

starving. Have you had dinner?" he asked Shari as she dragged another mat over.

She shook her head. "I haven't had time."

He glanced at his watch as he took the mat from her and shoved the last one into the storage area. "The sports bar is the only thing open now. Want to stop by there?"

Shari wiped the sweat from her face. The last time she'd been in a bar with a man, it had been with Simon. A resounding no was on the tip of her tongue, but when she glanced at Emmanuel, he looked as though he expected her to say exactly that. It wasn't the bar that she had problems with, after all. It had been the man she was with. What was that long self-lecture all about if she wasn't willing to reach out again?

Still, fear bubbled in the pit of her stomach. She remembered when she was a little girl and she was frightened of giving her first speech in class. She'd always been outtalked by her older siblings, and the experience had left her feeling inadequate. But though it felt like bees were stinging her midsection, she'd stood in front of the class—and bombed. It was the worst speech in the class. She'd been mortified and swore she'd never make another speech.

Her teacher had talked to her later that day. In her brisk manner she'd asked Shari to redo the speech. She had one week to prepare it again. She had told her teacher she couldn't do it. But Mrs. Butler had insisted.

Shari had worried that entire week. She couldn't eat. She spent nights preparing that speech—standing in her room, practicing behind a locked door. Still, when the day arrived, she was certain that she'd bomb again. But she hadn't. She hadn't stammered, she hadn't missed words. Her delivery had been perfect.

Recovering from rape hadn't been as easy. But she'd prepared herself. She'd taken the necessary steps to live a productive life. She was ready to go out again. Yet, she felt like that fifth grader who'd bombed out on that paper. But then, as now, she knew that one had to work through the fear.

"Sure," Shari finally said. "Just give me time to change clothes."

Emmanuel smiled. "You're fine," he said as he picked up her bag along with his and led the way to their cars.

She drove ahead of him to the bar. As she drove through the older section of town with stately homes on both sides of the road, all seemed quiet and at peace. Her brother had purchased a house in this neighborhood. The atmosphere was quite different when she reached the bar in downtown Nottoway. The music from inside spilled out, but it wouldn't leak so far as the residential district.

Several cars were parked in front. Emmanuel walked inside with her, his hand at the small of her back.

"Larger crowd than usual," he said. "Must be the overflow from the meeting."

He led her to one of the booths along the wall, and she settled into the seat as a waitress came over.

"What can I get you folks?" she asked.

"A menu," Emmanuel said.

She got two menus for them. "I missed the town meeting tonight."

"We didn't tell anyone anything more than what's in the papers," Emmanuel said.

"Sure is a shame about Claudia. Can I get you drinks while you wait?"

Emmanuel raised a brow at Shari. "A Sprite for me," she said.

"Iced coffee for me."

"Well, you don't plan to sleep tonight?"

Emmanuel shrugged. "I'm still on the job." Once the words had slipped, he thought better of them. He'd meant that once he left Shari, he had more work to do, but it hadn't come out that way. *You're losing your touch, old man.*

"That's what you call it now," the waitress said, and left to get their drinks, a smile on her face.

"The burgers are very good here," Emmanuel said.

"I think I want something lighter," Shari said as she perused the menu.

The waitress returned with their drinks.

"I'll have the chef salad," Shari said.

Emmanuel ordered the cheeseburger and handed the waitress his menu. He sat back in the booth and stared moodily at the woman before him as he sipped his coffee. He didn't have a clue as to why he'd asked her to dinner. She looked tired, as if she'd been missing sleep. But somehow her beauty still peeked through the dark circles beneath her eyes and the baggy clothing she wore. He'd give anything to see what Shari really looked like.

"Tell me how you got involved in self-defense," he asked her.

"I lived in the city. Women need skills on how to protect themselves."

He nodded but somehow he thought it was more than that. She was secretive. He wondered what course he should take to have her disclose her secrets.

"Claudia came by the Women's Center the week before she was murdered."

Emmanuel straightened. "She what?"

Shari sipped her drink and placed the glass on the coaster. "She came by the Center."

"Why?"

"I don't know. But she made an appointment with Dr. Snow. She picked up several brochures on the stand so I couldn't tell what she really needed."

Emmanuel took the notebook out of his pocket and jotted down the information. Something *was* going on. He only wished he knew what. Something that even her family and neighbors were unaware of. He wondered if Deborah knew. He'd have a talk with Dr. Snow tomorrow. Deborah was still out of town. He wondered if she knew of Claudia's death.

It seemed Emmanuel was destined to work more than fifteen hours each day. Once again he traveled the dark road to Claudia's house. Howard had been too distraught yesterday to be interviewed, but Emmanuel couldn't put it off any longer.

When he arrived, he saw three cars in the yard. Claudia's, her husband's, and one Emmanuel was unfamiliar with. Since the lights were still on, he felt no reservations about going there so late at night. As he exited his car and walked to the front door, he could hear the faint sound of a neighbor's dog barking two houses away. That was a good distance in this segment of the county. The dog was obviously tied to a leash and straining against it. Emmanuel rang the doorbell and waited.

Howard answered immediately and invited him in. He was dressed in jeans and a T-shirt. A young lady who looked to be Claudia's age sat on the family room couch. Two half-filled wineglasses were on the table. The woman's skirt reached more than halfway up her very shapely thighs. The scene struck Emmanuel as being wrong somehow. It was almost as if the woman and Howard were courting. It went against the grain when a man courted before his wife was even buried. But then again, Emmanuel could be reading the situation entirely wrong. He didn't know the woman, after all.

"I would like to ask you a few questions," he said to Howard.

"It couldn't wait until after the funeral?" Howard asked.

Emmanuel shook his head. "Afraid not. I've waited longer than I should have as it is."

The woman stood, smoothing out her tight skirt. "I have to be leaving anyway. Howard, I'm so sorry for your loss. I'll be in touch."

"It was good of you to come by. Let me walk you to the car."

She waved a hand and shook her head. "I can see myself out." Then she glanced at Emmanuel. "It's nice to meet you, Officer."

"Emmanuel Jones," he said. "And you are . . . ?"

"Saffron Jackson."

Emmanuel stored the information. "I hope you don't have far to drive," he said.

"Not too far. Just to Richmond."

"A pleasure meeting you."

Emmanuel remembered Howard's company had said that he was in Richmond on business the day Claudia died. The woman hugged Howard, and he walked her to the door, closing it after her. There was more going on here than simply an acquaintance visiting the bereaved.

Howard returned to the room. "Can I get you some wine?"

Emmanuel shook his head and pulled out a small notebook. "I just have a few questions to ask."

"Well, have a seat first. This isn't the big city. We're friendly here."

Emmanuel eased himself into the sofa cushion. "But this is official business."

"I understand. Do you have a clue on who killed Claudia?" he asked with a worried frown on his face. "I can't sleep in the bedroom knowing what happened."

"We're still checking out leads."

"Somebody said it could be that serial killer in Petersburg."

"As soon as we have the autopsy report, we'll know." Emmanuel turned a few pages in his notebook and took his pen from his breast pocket. He wrote "Saffron Jackson" on the pad and dated it.

Howard sprawled in the chair across from him.

"Where were you the day of the murder?"

"I left for Richmond at five-thirty, like I usually do. I had a six-thirty delivery."

"Can you verify that?"

"Yeah. All the paperwork is at the office. You can

get the name of the person who signed for the delivery to verify my whereabouts."

Emmanuel added that to the information on his pad. "Was your wife worried about anything? Did she feel a sense of danger or act strangely in the last few weeks?"

"Not as far as I know. She didn't mention anything to me if she was. You know Claudia. Thinks she can take care of everything herself. She's got the independent spirit."

"Has anything unusual happened in the last few weeks?"

Again Howard shook his head. "Nope. I'm thinking it might be that serial killer everybody's so worried about."

Emmanuel glanced up at him. Why was he trying to convince him it was the serial killer? Was it to lead the suspicion away from himself? "Why would you think that?"

"They said she was tied up when she was found."

Emmanuel nodded and asked a few more questions. Howard didn't seem to be a man who felt bereaved. A wife should be missed, regardless of the state of the relationship. Emmanuel was aware that people expressed their loss in different ways, but usually there was something to indicate a sense of loss. Or maybe he was just measuring this all wrong.

Emmanuel carried a sense of guilt himself. He should have forced Claudia to speak to him immediately. He shouldn't have waited the way she wanted him to. Then, too, who was he to force her to do anything? But if he had, she might be alive right now.

Emmanuel glanced at Howard again. Could he have killed his wife for money or to begin his life with someone new? Perhaps even the woman who just left?

After the questioning, Emmanuel left. More questions had been raised than answered. It was ten-thirty. The autopsy was scheduled for tomorrow morning.

Chapter 4

"You really are gorgeous in that dress," Clarice said as soon as she saw Shari. "I told you pearls would set it off. Though why you bought your own instead of borrowing mine puzzles me. Never mind." She waved a hand and dropped a tote bag on the sofa. "If things turn out the way we've planned, then you'll be wearing them a lot."

"It's a simple, mandatory date. That's all," Shari assured her sister, but didn't think that Clarice listened—she heard only what she wanted to.

The dinner Shari had shared with Emmanuel still plagued her. Most of all, her conflicting emotions for the man confused her. He'd done nothing to lead her on, it was just *her*—that magnetic pull and unease. Was it noticeable? Could Clarice and Johanna detect her reaction to Emmanuel? Had that been the reason they bid such an outrageous amount for him?

Gosh, she hoped not. Because if they could detect her unspoken attraction, then perhaps Emmanuel could, too. He already had too many notches on his post.

"Hello!" Johanna Blake called from the kitchen door, her face all but pressed against the screen.

Clarice turned. "Hi, there. What're you doing here?"

"Same as you," Johanna said, carrying another tote bag as she entered the house, and then she stopped. "Is this Shari? Oh, my God. You look like a new person. Oh, girl, you're going to sweep my poor brother off his feet."

"Oh, pul-lease," Shari said. "You act like I've never been on a date before."

"Not dressed like that—since you moved here anyway. My brother's done for."

Shari rolled her eyes toward the ceiling. "You two need to go home. I don't need the whole family here for the occasion."

"We're taking pictures," Clarice said. Both women took cameras out of their tote bags and wagged them in the air.

"No, you aren't. You're leaving." Shari grabbed each woman by the arm and hustled them toward the door. Midway there, the doorbell rang. Could this day get any worse?

"Emmanuel's here!" Clarice said. The women were as excited as mothers sending off their daughters on prom night.

Shari groaned. "I can't wait for your daughters to be old enough to date."

"Until then, we have you." Clarice moved out of Shari's grasp.

"No, you don't. Just take your cameras and leave." She pointed an imperious finger at the side door as she rushed to the front door, smoothing her dress and stopping long enough to pause by the foyer mirror to make sure everything was in place. She wasn't looking cool. She schooled her expression to indifference and turned back to glance at her uninvited guests. Clarice and Johanna were watching her. She sighed and opened the door.

"Hello. Is Shari in?" Emmanuel checked his watch.

Shari glanced at the long white stretch limo behind him and frowned. "Oh, don't be cute." She pushed the screen open and marched to the family room where Clarice and Johanna were snapping pictures.

Emmanuel sighed and caught the door before it slammed in his face. She must be one of Shari's snippy sisters. But darn if she didn't have a cute backside . . . and legs . . . and bust—everything Shari was missing. He forgot for a second how much Shari was wearing on him.

"Hi!"

"What is this?" *Jesus. Women.* A brother couldn't go on a date quietly. Women had to bring the whole choir to see them off.

"We want pictures."

Emmanuel looked across the room at the sister with her arms crossed over her breasts. After a few seconds he realized it was Shari. He blinked and tried to compose his expression. He lifted the box in his hand and carried it over to her. Thinking that this was probably her first date in years, he'd thought he should be kind to her. Now he felt silly carrying the corsage in his hand. He opened the box and took out the expensive arrangement.

"Ah, isn't that cute?" Johanna said.

"Sure is," Clarice agreed.

"Don't," Emmanuel and Shari started together.

Emmanuel leveled a look at them, which they ignored. "Don't you have families to see to?"

"Not tonight. Our husbands are taking care of everything."

Emmanuel shook his head in consternation. Men were destined to have a hard time today. Every time he turned around, the men were baby-sitting.

"We're leaving as soon as we get pictures," Clarice said.

Emmanuel turned back to Shari. He took in the curve of her breast displayed by the low-cut dress and tried to be cool as he reached for the strap to pin the corsage. He thanked the stars he'd opted against the wrist corsage.

"I'll do it," Shari muttered as she lifted a hand to take the corsage from him.

"Let him do it. It's a date." Clarice held the camera to her eye.

"I can get it done faster."

Johanna hummed. "Live with the moment, girlfriend. We've got to get pictures of him pinning it."

"And please try to look happy, not like he's about to stab you," Clarice said.

"As soon as you get this picture, you're leaving," Emmanuel told the women.

"Remember, it's all for charity. We'll put pictures of all the couples in the Women's Center. So look happy."

He watched Shari school a fake happy expression on her face. She jerked a bit when he tried once again to pin the corsage in place. He was a pro at pinning the things, but her agitation was making him nervous. He felt her warm, soft skin against the back of his fingers as he held the corsage in place and guided the pin. Then he stepped back in satisfaction. It was perfectly aligned. He'd chosen white since he didn't have a clue as to what she'd wear. He was pleased with the outcome. Although she usually looked like the virginal type, right now she looked far from virginal.

"I have something for you, too." She stepped away and went to the refrigerator. Emmanuel enjoyed the view of her slim back exposed by the dress. She retrieved a small box and took out the boutonniere. She made quick work of attaching it to his lapel as Clarice and Johanna continued to snap pictures.

"Okay, we want pictures in the living room."

Both of them frowned, but like high school prom dates, they marched to the living room and stood in front of the fireplace while the ladies took pictures to their satisfaction.

"Okay, you've got enough pictures for your bulletin board."

"This is for family, too."

"You can make copies," Shari snapped as she retrieved her black silk jacket from the closet.

She and Clarice played tug-of-war with the jacket. "It's cool on the boat," she whispered.

"It's ninety degrees outside," Clarice said quietly to her, but not so that Emmanuel didn't hear.

"An air conditioner is an invention that is used quite frequently," Shari said with a smile. "Inside the temperature will be closer to seventy."

"Then get Emmanuel to keep you warm." She snatched the jacket out of Shari's arm and handed her a skimpy shawl. It was just for show. There wasn't enough to keep a flea warm. Shari took it from her and turned back to Emmanuel with a false smile. "Ready?"

"Sure." He contained a smile as he held the door for her. Johanna and Clarice piled out behind them, snapping pictures of the white stretch limousine.

After the couple slid onto the plush seats, the ladies returned to the house.

"Sorry about that," Shari said.

Emmanuel lifted a champagne bottle and popped the cork. "Nothing to apologize for. Let's just have a good time tonight—as friends."

Shari measured him as if she didn't trust him. "Just friends," she repeated.

"Let's toast." He poured champagne in two glasses.

"Sure." She took the glass he offered her. They clicked and sipped the expensive brand—compliments of Johanna. A tray of fresh strawberries dipped in chocolate and an arrangement of cheese, crackers and French bread had also been provided.

Emmanuel was starved and offered to fill a plate for her, but she declined. He fixed one for himself and he ate his fill as he tried to think of conversation to last them the two-hour drive to Norfolk. His stomach was still queasy from the autopsy yesterday, but he hadn't eaten all day, and he was starving. Still, he felt odd eating alone. He picked up a strawberry from the container and fed it to Shari. He was surprised when she opened her mouth and bit into the luscious fruit.

A vaguely sensuous light passed between them. His heart jolted and his pulse pounded. Shari reached for a plate and the spell was broken. She began to loosen up a bit. He tried not to look at her cleavage—at least when he did peek, he managed to do it in such a way that she couldn't detect it.

His sudden attraction to this woman mystified him. It was an attraction he didn't want, especially since it began through the maneuvering of his sister.

Soft light illuminated them as they stood on the deck of *The Spirit of Norfolk*. The wind blew gently and the temperature had dropped. Emmanuel gently draped the shawl around Shari's shoulders and left his arm in place.

She stiffened and glanced up questioningly at him.

"Relax," he said. "Clarice was wrong. It is cool."

"Well, don't tell her that," Shari said, looking out into the Atlantic. "Big sisters are never wrong."

Emmanuel chuckled, thinking of Pam and Johanna. "Don't I know it." He needed this. The last few days had been a whirlwind. Shari relaxed a little, but she was still a little stiff.

"Why did you choose investigating as a career? Policemen get a bad rap now, and in many cases, they deserve it."

"Policemen don't have to be bad. We're in the perfect position to do good in the neighborhoods. If good men and women don't become policemen then what's left?"

"Hmmm," Shari said. "You've got a point there. But what inspired you?"

"Gardell Gaines and I have been friends since high school. So I ended up spending a lot of time at his place and he at mine. His dad was sheriff, so I got to see a lot of what goes on in police departments, the kind of work they do, the unfairness."

"Gaines. That name seems familiar."

"It should be. He's the man who tried to kill your sister ten years ago."

"You're kidding! And this man was responsible for you becoming a policeman?"

"I never saw that side of him before."

"So the new detective is his son."

"Yeah. Gardell's a good detective. His father was weak, but he has more of his mother's strength."

"I see."

Emmanuel shifted his arm around her. Suddenly he wanted to kiss her neck. "Do you?" What was it about this snippy woman that turned him on? She was the exact opposite of the women who usually attracted him. In the past he'd liked relationships which a man didn't have to work very hard to maintain.

"How long have you been an investigator?"

"Five years. When the last detective retired, I took his place." She had relaxed somewhat, but now she was tense again. Emmanuel wondered if she felt that same magnetism that ate at him.

"How did you actually get on the force?"

"I went directly to the police academy. After that I took courses at Virginia State." He didn't want to talk about work when the urge to kiss her drove him crazy. He cleared his throat. The soft music inside spilled out on deck, creating a romantic mood, which was enhanced by the view of the harbor across the water. Was it the music and the ambiance, or was it this strange attraction building between them? It seemed to grow stronger each time they met. "Shari?" His mouth felt thick.

"Yes?"

"Let's go inside," he whispered.

She turned to glance at him, and he lowered his head to kiss her. Her response shocked him. He expected her to pull away, but as he lifted his arms and tightened them around her, pressing her to him, he felt her hands on his back.

The sweet, soft texture of her lips drove his heart wild. Feasting on her was better than dessert. His libido was taking him places his mind wasn't ready to explore—but his body definitely was, he thought as he moved his tongue gently over her lips.

Just a little taste, he promised himself as he thrust his tongue between her lips. He wanted to say the hell with propriety and take his fill. As his tongue explored the recesses of her mouth, the thought that she was off-limits did nothing to dampen the desire riding him like a wave. The kiss sent a wild swirl into the pit of his stomach. He was intrigued at the paradox of the woman with the shapeless clothes, who was cautious to a fault, yet who let him kiss her. He wanted to know all her secrets—to touch her skin beneath the shawl. He pulled the shawl from her shoulders and smoothed his hands over her bare skin.

For a moment heat flowed through his body and settled in his midsection. This was crazy. He tore his lips from hers and leaned his forehead against hers. "We can't do this," he whispered.

Her hand stroked his back. "No, we can't."

He kissed her forehead tenderly. And touched her mouth briefly. Her lips were still warm and moist from his kiss. Her shawl had dropped to the deck, so he picked it up and he placed it tenderly around her shoulders. With his hand at the small of her back, he guided her inside to the dance floor. Maybe the exertion would cool his body.

The bachelor auction had already changed his life. Somehow he felt differently about Shari.

Emmanuel stood at the balcony railing of his hotel room the next morning sipping his first cup of coffee as he gazed out at the Atlantic Ocean. Several joggers ran along the shore. Some stopped to gather seashells. The wind was brisk, the air thick and salty.

He wondered if Shari was up yet. Probably, he thought. She wasn't one to dawdle.

After their kiss on deck last night, he'd left her at her hotel door and disappeared into his room. He'd been afraid to touch her since there seemed to be nothing to stop them from exploring his desire. He only knew that as much as she intrigued him, she wasn't the one for him. So why did the image of her in a bathing suit appeal to him so intently?

He glanced at his watch. He could smell the salt spray. It was warm, not too hot. The water seemed to beckon him. It would be a shame to come to Virginia Beach and not take advantage of the ocean. Before he could stop himself, he picked up the phone and dialed Shari's room.

"Let's go for a swim," Emmanuel said when she answered.

"I thought you needed to get back."

"When was the last time you had a vacation?"

"Before I came to Nottoway," she said hesitantly.

"That long, hmm?" Most people lived for vacations.

"It doesn't seem that long."

Emmanuel knew his schedule would be a killer once they returned to Nottoway. He may as well make the best of their excursion. "We have time for a swim and breakfast. I'll meet you at your door in fifteen minutes." If he gave her too much time, she'd be primping all morning if she were anything like his sister Pam.

He called the office to ask Gardell for an update. The medical examiner hadn't released any additional information but Gardell said something about the findings had puzzled him. Emmanuel was eager to discover what it was.

He forced himself to block out the case while he slid into his swim trunks, grabbed a couple of towels, and headed to Shari's room. It was difficult to do, but he owed Shari that much.

As he opened the door, he saw a multicolored sarong wrapped around her shapely bottom and a towel in her hand.

"Sleep well?" he asked as they made their way to the beach.

"Just fine. You?" Her hair flowed freely around her shoulders making her appear younger than when she wore it in the bun.

He hadn't slept well at all. Most of the night, when he wasn't thinking about the case, he thought about what lay beneath that green dress.

They arrived at the beach and he peeled off the shorts he wore over his bathing suit. "We'll leave our things here," he said and dropped the shorts and towels in a pile. Shari untied her sarong and folded it neatly, laying it on top of the towels. Her bathing suit was one piece, but there was something to be said for the shape beneath. The sister had shape enough to make him drool.

Emmanuel either had to have her or do something to expend some energy.

As they ran into the ocean, the cold Atlantic hit them like a chilly slap. He pulled Shari out into chest-high water. It was either kiss her or toss her. He tossed her. She came up sputtering, eyes wide with shock. Then she dived underneath and caught his legs. Unexpectedly he found himself sinking to the bottom. When he found his feet, he charged after her. The game was on.

Shari had lived near the ocean all her life. She wasn't about to be bested by some land person. She took off like a shark, dodging his attacks, letting him get only so close and taking off again. Then she let him catch her. She found herself lifted into the air and dunked like a ball. She sank, but when she went after his legs again they weren't anywhere in sight. Then she felt him from behind as he lifted her and dropped her again. It was totally unexpected when he caught her again and brought her up against his chest. Their breathing was labored. His body was wet and slick against hers and goose bumps began to spread along her skin where it was exposed above the water. Was she getting chilled or was it Emmanuel?

The smile left Emmanuel's face as his lips neared hers. Then he kissed her. His kiss was frenzied as his hands fell to her behind and he ground his length against her. His lips were salty and cool—his mouth piercingly hot. An electrical jolt pierced through Shari as she cupped the back of his head and pressed closer to him. The bulge in his trunks pressed against her stomach.

"You feel so right in my arms," he whispered against her ear as he trailed stinging kisses along her face.

"Oh, yeah," Shari said. The world slowly came into focus. The sound of children shrieking pierced her desire.

Emmanuel pulled back from her and stood for a moment just gazing at her. Then he drew his tongue over his lips and blew out a long breath. "Are you ready for breakfast?"

Shari nodded. She thought she'd just had breakfast.

They left the water and he gave her a towel to dry off. Shari realized that she didn't fear him, but was she ready for this? Were his kisses real? It was difficult to remind herself that Emmanuel was a player. He was accustomed to pleasuring women, while her relationships in the past had been more serious. She may be ready to lead a full life again, but she wasn't prepared for an affair. Any relationship with Emmanuel would only be temporary.

After a buffet breakfast at the hotel, Shari talked to her parents on the phone, then she and Emmanuel took the limousine back to Nottoway in splendid luxury. They arrived in town around one on Sunday afternoon.

As soon as Emmanuel reached home, he changed and went directly to Claudia's parents' home. He welcomed the work to clear his fevered images of Shari from his mind.

He had tried to interview them before, but all he could gather was that they were convinced Howard was a murderer. Still they had no proof. Emmanuel sighed. He'd give it another shot and see if they offered any helpful information.

"How are you, Mrs. Anderson?" he asked once he'd settled into a chair and she'd handed him lemonade.

"I tell you, Emmanuel, I don't think I'll ever recover." She rubbed her tear-streaked face with a tissue and Emmanuel left his seat to gather her in his arms. "I wanted to go to church today, but I just couldn't handle being around so many people," she mumbled against his chest. Mrs. Anderson was a devout Baptist. She attended church regularly along with Mrs. Drucilla and his mama.

"First time she missed church this year," Claudia's aunt Bernice said.

"It's been a blow, Emmanuel." Mr. Anderson walked in and sank wearily into a chair.

Mrs. Anderson went to the kitchen table, and sat down. Emmanuel smelled the food cooking on the stove, even though the counter was filled with dishes neighbors and friends had delivered. That Sunday ritual was the familiar.

"Come on, sit down, Emmanuel," Mrs. Anderson said, pointing to the chair at the end of the table.

Emmanuel took the chair, but it was times like these that he most disliked. He wished he could just visit with these folks for a while, but he was here not only as a family friend but also as a detective.

"Can I get you something, Emmanuel?" Claudia's aunt asked. "We've got chicken, ham—a whole table full of food. There's plenty to share. Mrs. Drucilla dropped off some of her barbecue this morning."

"The lemonade hits the spot, thanks." Then he focused on the sad couple beside him.

"I hate to have to bother you right now, but I need answers to some questions."

"Go ahead." Mrs. Anderson crumpled the soggy napkin in her hand and shook her head. "You've got to put that husband of hers away. We'll help you any way we can."

"He was always no good," Mr. Anderson lamented. "She shoulda left him a long time ago."

"You still believe that he killed Claudia?"

"Who else would do such a thing?" Mrs. Anderson's mouth tightened into a straight line.

"Do you have anything that would prove it?"

"Because when he started dating that new woman, he changed. He was mean to Claudia." Her mouth trembled.

Her husband put his hand on hers and patted it. "Been bold about his dating, too. He used to hide his doings, but they've been seen together all around Richmond."

"Shamed my daughter something fierce until she had no recourse but to divorce him."

"And that's why he killed her," Mr. Anderson said. "He's going to get all that insurance money. My daughter is dead and he's rich."

"You'll make sure he pays for it, won't you, Emmanuel?" Mrs. Anderson watched him with a weary strain on her face.

The fact that they were talking about Claudia getting a divorce surprised him. "We're going to do our best to find the killer, whoever it is," he said. "We'll look into the insurance."

She pointed an imperious finger at him. "You take care of your business any way you see fit. But I'm telling you it's *him*." Her mouth tightened. "You were always kind to Claudia. She said you were the best man she'd ever dated. I thought you'd get married." She shook her head sadly. "But it just didn't work out that way. It wasn't meant to be."

Emmanuel sat speechless. He and Claudia had been high school sweethearts a long time ago. They'd been so young.

"The funeral's tomorrow. You're coming, aren't you?"

"I'll be there," he said.

She'd deserved a lot better than Howard or him, Emmanuel thought as he sipped his drink. He thought that if Claudia *had* asked Howard for a divorce, and if he'd threatened her, then perhaps that was what she'd wanted to talk to him about. But why did she need to see a therapist? He wished so many times that he'd insisted that they meet right away.

Emmanuel finished his drink, thanked them for the information, and left.

When he passed the road that led to Shari's, he thought of her many questions at the town meeting. Then he began to think about the clothing she wore—the baggy, unrevealing attire and the beautiful dress she'd worn Saturday night. On the drive back to Nottoway, she'd once again donned her usual attire. Again he wondered if she'd been molested at some time in her life.

He'd thought that the evening with her would be

long and boring, but she was well versed in many areas. He'd actually enjoyed himself, and found himself feeling their time together had been far too short. He realized he'd like to take her out again, but he hated his sister's interference. Then, too, Shari was a for-keeps kind of woman, not a for-now woman. He still wasn't ready for that kind of relationship. He was definitely a for-now man. Truth be told, he was tired of meaningless relationships. Not that he wanted children. God knows there were plenty in his family. Six between his two sisters. But his dad was worried that the family name wouldn't be carried on. And the responsibility of that weighed heavily on Emmanuel's shoulders. There was that tradition and family responsibility that had been hammered in him from the time he could remember.

But Emmanuel couldn't stand to live in a house like the one he'd grown up in. His sisters and mother were constantly at war—especially Johanna and Mom. He'd go outside sometimes just to get away from the fighting. Now he loved his peaceful home. Not that the one-bedroom cottage he'd built a few years ago was anything to brag about, but he had only one bedroom for a reason. He didn't want any relatives staying overnight. His only exception was the nieces and nephews who stayed over now and then. He could tolerate them because it wasn't that often. He loved his peace. That was why he never shacked up with a woman.

The family Sunday dinner was held at his mom's house. The family had grown so large after Johanna married Jonathan, that the dining room wouldn't accommodate everyone, so Jonathan, James and Emmanuel had built another dining room onto the house. The three of them were always building something together. His sisters had chosen husbands well. But today they'd be eating on the back porch the three of them had built a couple of years back. And thank goodness they'd installed two ceiling fans.

He fingered the shawl Shari had left in the car. Before he could stop himself, he was headed in the direction of her home. His excuse was that he needed to return the shawl to her. The reality was he wanted to see her again. *Emmanuel, you're a fool. You just parted a couple of hours ago.*

It was a quiet day at Shari's house. Because of her date with Emmanuel, she hadn't brought work home with her this weekend.

Clarice had invited her to Sunday dinner, but Shari begged off and offered to keep the children until dinner.

They were eight and six, the older being a boy. She enjoyed being with them.

Right now they were playing a math game on the computer.

"We're tired of playing this, Aunt Shari. You got anything interesting for us to play—like Nintendo?"

Shari didn't believe in Nintendo and the other foolish games kids zoned out on. There were plenty of fun educational games for them to play—plenty of learning sites for them to explore. "Why don't we surf the Net for some new things?"

Both children groaned.

"It's summertime. We play during the summer, Aunt Shari. Summers are for breaks from work."

"Your mind doesn't have to go to mush during the summer."

"I want to see Disney," Chantel said.

"We can always go for a walk and explore." She thought of the murderer. "On second thought, why don't . . ." A car door slammed.

"Somebody's here!" Both children hopped from the computer and ran to the door. Their faces fell when they saw it wasn't their father.

"Hey, what's with you two?" Emmanuel asked.

"We're bored. Aunt Shari won't let us do any fun stuff on her computer."

"And we want to go play," Chantel whined.

Emmanuel smiled and looked at Shari over the children's head. "Why don't the four of us go outside for a while?" He figured that between Jonathan, James, and his father, his mother's household was fine.

"Oh, great!" They charged off and began to look for their sneakers.

Emmanuel held up the shawl. "You forgot something. Thought I'd bring it by. You may need it for something."

She walked toward him and took it. "Thank you."

"My pleasure." She was dressed in loose-fitting cotton slacks with a drawstring at the waist and a short-sleeved baggy shirt. "I hope you don't mind—about the walk."

"It's a little late for that, isn't it? I couldn't keep them in with restraints now."

"It's okay to go outside, you know. Just be aware of your surroundings."

"I'm not afraid to go outside."

Chantel finally unearthed her sneakers and slid them on. Then they went outside.

"Let's take a walk toward the lake," Emmanuel said. The kids hopped and skipped in front of them. Emmanuel adjusted his pace to Shari's.

"I'd like to see you again," he said quietly so the kids wouldn't hear.

"We had our outing as a benefit to the Women's Center, Emmanuel. But your reputation precedes you. I don't want to be involved with a man whom I know will end the relationship after he tires of me in a few months. I'd just be one in a million for you."

"You're exaggerating."

"But you know what I mean."

"No one knows what the future will bring. We can't live our lives anticipating problems."

"But we already know there isn't a future for us."

Emmanuel sighed. Maybe she was right. They shouldn't start something that would end so soon, but being with her just felt too . . . right. He wanted to explore—to find out where this could lead. But if his feelings weren't reciprocated, then what was the point?

Chapter 5

From the time Emmanuel was a child, he'd hated funerals. Since becoming an adult, that hadn't changed. Emmanuel selected his black suit for the service. Somehow the loss didn't seem real until after the viewing of the body and the closing of the casket, even though he looked at the photographs of Claudia's dead body in her investigation file many times each day.

Nottoway Baptist was a large church situated on a wooded lot that seemed to be in the middle of nowhere. The white wooden building had originally been constructed in the late 1800s. Some ancestor of Emmanuel's had been one of the founding members. With the influx of more people into Nottoway as Jonathan's company grew, the town was now able to keep many of its college graduates. The membership at the church had increased so that three years ago the building had been expanded. Now the brick structure, with its tall steeple, had flowers growing in the center of a well-cut lawn. People trampled the grass as they conversed out front.

He left the car and started toward the building. He'd taken no more than two steps when he heard, "Hey, Emmanuel."

He stopped and glanced in the direction of the voice. Deborah Hines tiptoed toward him, trying to keep her heels from sinking into the gravel. He waved and waited for her. She was slightly plump and wore a black dress that reached just below her knees. Her red eyes flaunted the effects of a recent crying jag.

"I just wanted a word with you about Claudia," she said, catching her breath and dabbing at the sweat gathering on her forehead.

"How are you, Deborah?" he asked.

"It's tough, Emmanuel." She looked ready to collapse. "She was my best friend in the world. We'd call each other about silly things—about work, after a long shift when something happened at the hospital or her office. I miss her so much. She always understood."

Words were inadequate to describe this kind of loss, and Emmanuel didn't even try. He merely put his arms around her and held her, letting her pour out her grief. Emmanuel stroked her arm until the sobbing lessened. The soggy tissue in her hand shredded and Emmanuel felt his breast pocket for one of the handkerchiefs his mom still bought him every Christmas.

"What is it you wanted to tell me?" he said finally when she was able to speak.

"I don't know if you know this or not, and I hate

to have to tell you this on today of all days, but I think you need to know." She sniffed and blew her nose. "Claudia has been dating some guy over the Internet."

"Do you know who?"

She shook her head. "But he must live nearby. They were supposed to meet that day in the park— around eleven-thirty. Just for a half hour, you know. I told her it was dangerous. But she was convinced he was nice. She'd already asked Howard for a divorce." She glanced toward the limousines that brought the family to the church and frowned when she recognized Howard behind the dark glasses. She turned back to Emmanuel. "His womanizing hurt her real bad. I should have gone with her, and I would have, too, if I were here. I had to go out of town. I tried to get her to promise to wait until I returned, but she wouldn't."

"She died long before eleven-thirty when they'd planned to meet."

"You think he discovered where she lived? Maybe he was a predator. Somebody said she wasn't killed in the park."

"That's something we'll investigate."

"Well, I've got to get on in." She touched Emmanuel's arm, then looked at the waddled hankie.

"Keep it," Emmanuel said.

"I'll talk to you later," she said, and hurried to the church.

Emmanuel stood near his car and watched the people arriving for the funeral, wondering if any of the men could have been Claudia's computer date. He pulled the ever-present notebook out of his breast pocket and wrote the date and time at the top, then jotted down the new information Deborah had volunteered. He'd barely tucked the book away when he saw Shari's car drive up and park near the road. She checked herself in the mirror, patted her hair, and ran a powder puff over her face before she exited the car.

Emmanuel smiled. She wore a shapeless black dress with a long-sleeved matching jacket and she must be burning her up in this ninety-degree weather. Emmanuel looked again. The dress hung just a few inches above her serviceable, closed-in black pumps. But she looked as cool as a cucumber.

He strolled in her direction. "Mind if I sit with you?" Emmanuel asked.

She glanced at him sideways. "You keep turning up like a bad penny."

"I'm hoping to wear on you." He wondered what it would take to bring back the sexy, carefree woman of the weekend? Someone had to take this woman in hand, or else she'd never learn the pleasures of life. Whatever she'd been through, he planned to gently help her over the trauma. Emmanuel guided her with a hand around her elbow. She jumped and narrowed her eyes at him. He stared straight ahead as though his gesture was natural. She sighed and then relaxed. Her skin beneath the jacket was warm against his touch. The faint scent of her perfume waffled delicately in the air.

"I wasn't aware that you knew Claudia that well," Emmanuel said as he watched his sister smiling at them from across the yard as she walked beside her husband. They'd left the children home with the nanny.

"She and I worked on the Women's Center committee together for a while. We're planning a memorial fund in her name. Are you making any progress with the investigation?"

"Some."

Shari discreetly tugged against his hold.

Emmanuel held on.

"I thought we agreed," she said.

"Not that I'm aware of. Oh. I forgot. We agreed to be friends." He nudged her on. "You're not being very friendly. Maybe I can help you with that," he said as he perused the crowd. "I guess we better get inside. It's almost time for the service."

She stopped tugging, gave him the eye sisters learn almost from birth, and walked sedately along with him.

Emmanuel stood with Shari at the gravesite. He surveyed the grounds, looking for strangers. There were plenty today. Many were relatives who had come in from Baltimore, New York, and North Carolina. There were also coworkers and friends. Claudia was a very likable woman. The vast arrangements of flowers by the graveside attested to that. Family and friends were picking some of the pretty blossoms for memory.

In some circles it was customary to give the flowers to hospitals or donate the money one would have spent on flowers to the victim's favorite charities. But many felt that life itself dealt a hard blow and the least one could do was give the deceased a good send-off. They could donate to the charity of their choosing during their lifetime.

People were beginning to leave for the reception at

Claudia's home. *I have to stop thinking of it as Claudia's,*
Emmanuel thought. The house belonged to Howard
now. He glanced at the man still sitting in a chair
under the awning. Men with shovels waited for the
family to leave so they could cover the grave. Several
single women consoled Howard, patting his hand,
leaving their lipstick behind on his cheek after their
kisses, and the scent of their perfumed bodies after
their hugs, all of them telling him they were available
for anything he might need, Emmanuel thought.

Emmanuel's mother wandered over to where he,
Shari, and Johanna stood. She eyed Shari closely and
then greeted her.

"Like a pack of hounds fighting over a meaty
bone," she complained, looking after Howard. She'd
changed from her heels into black flats. She'd said
she was tired of having her heels ruined in the dirt.
"Claudia's body isn't even in the grave yet and they're
hitting on him already. God rest her soul." She
squinted after another woman who offered condo-
lences. "I hope they don't disrespect me so when
I'm gone."

"Don't even talk like that, Mama," Emmanuel said.
Even though he planned to check out the information Deborah had given him, he still hadn't dis-
counted Howard. It was true Howard had one-
hundred-thousand-dollars in insurance money coming to him and the mortgage was paid off. The new
girlfriend and Claudia's threat of divorce were plenty
of incentives.

His mom touched his arm. "Yeah, baby. I know
you'll look out for me."

Johanna rolled her eyes.

Emmanuel briefly closed his eyes. He was thirty—

stood at six-three beside the woman he was trying to court—and his mama still called him baby. He was going to have a long talk with her.

"Don't worry. Daddy loves you, Mama," Johanna said. "You don't have to worry about other women."

Gladys looked fondly at her husband who was standing with a group of men across the way. "I've been lucky in choosing a husband, that's for sure. I'd just like to think he'll mourn me for a little while at least."

"I wish you wouldn't talk about death. We'll all miss you."

She patted Emmanuel's hands.

Their dad came over. "You're the famous computer expert Jonathan's always raving about," he said to Shari.

Shari smiled. "I don't know about famous."

"He speaks highly of you." Then he looked at the people milling about. "It's a darn shame." He sighed. "You ready, Gladys?"

That seemed to be the signal for everyone to disperse. They first gave their respects to Claudia's parents, but it took a while to get near Howard.

Then Emmanuel walked Shari to her car and opened the door for her as she slid in. "A new movie is showing Friday night. I'd like to see it with you."

"You're carrying it a bit far, don't you think? You don't have to do this just because my sister and yours set up this bachelor date."

"My asking you has nothing to do with them."

"Umm, I don't think so. We've already talked about it, remember? I don't want . . ."

"You enjoyed yourself this weekend, I hope." His voice turned low and sexy. "I know I did."

Shari's heart hammered in her chest. "Yes, I did, but . . ."

He tapped the car and started backing away. "Pick you up at five-thirty? We can go to the early show and have dinner at Karina's restaurant afterward."

Shari shoved open the door. "Absolutely not. I usually work late."

"You can get off early one night, can't you? Unless you have something against me? Have I insulted you—mistreated you? I know I'm a workaholic, but even I need to take time out now and then. So do you." He approached her again—put his arm on the roof of the car and bent close to her.

Shari had trouble thinking coherently. Being a hardworking woman herself, she could appreciate a hardworking man.

"Emmanuel, you can find any number of women to take out. Why me?"

That lopsided grin she was coming to like too much played around the corners of his mouth. "Because I enjoy your company."

She thought about eating popcorn in the dark, drinking sodas and sitting there with his arm brushing against hers or his arm around her shoulder, the spicy aroma of his cologne—and loving all of it. She then glanced six months in the future when he'd had his fill of her. "No. I have too much work to do."

Someone called Emmanuel's name. "See you at five-thirty," he said to her as he shut the door and left.

She opened the door a crack. "I said no." She was still tingling from being near him for the last couple of hours. As soon as he learned her fear of intimacy, he'd be on to the next woman—he'd be disappointed, disgusted. She wasn't going to set herself up for that again. Going through it once was painful enough. But setting her up and feeling that he wasn't the type to be patient enough for her to learn to trust him was ludicrous. Sure she enjoyed his kisses, but a long stretch separated kisses from deeper intimacy.

Shari turned the ignition key and found a small space to turn around to go back down the narrow dirt path that led away from the cemetery.

Yes, she enjoyed his company. She kind of wanted to see him again. He was wonderful with the children. He'd be disappointed in her.

When did you become so self-conscious, Shari? Where was that confidence that was drummed into you from before you could remember? Are you going to let one incident in your life—albeit a life-altering event—change you from the person you are? And for how long? Was all that therapy for naught?

Shari sighed. Those were some hard-hitting questions she was going to have to deal with, she thought as she decided to go directly back to the office.

Emmanuel had hoped for some positive leads before Claudia's funeral. Claudia's computer friend was another good lead. But Claudia didn't seem to be the kind of person to while away her time in chat rooms. She was a people person—she liked doing, mingling, not sitting at a computer in her solitary office.

She must have been lonely those Friday and Saturday nights that Howard spent socializing with other women. And she must have hated those pitying looks from family and friends who knew the score.

Claudia was a one-man woman. She never would have agreed to see another man unless she'd ended it with her husband. Emmanuel knew from past experience that she didn't dawdle. Once she'd made a decision, that was it. There wouldn't be a reconciliation. If she had asked Howard for a divorce, she'd basically ended it there and felt that she could move on. He wondered if she'd talked with a lawyer. There were only a few around town. He'd make some calls.

Emmanuel glanced at Howard again then looked off to the side where two women stood. One was the woman who was at Howard's house the night he interviewed him. It seemed odd that a friend of his from Richmond would attend the wife's funeral. Emmanuel wondered about the identity of the woman who stood with her. Howard's mother had spoken to her earlier. But no one else at the funeral seemed to know her.

Another lone figure stood with Jonathan. He'd seen the man around town, but didn't know him. Emmanuel wondered if the man worked at Blake Industries.

Johanna and Karina were talking to Clarice and her brother Gerald, who was one of the finest lawyers in the town. He'd call his office later that day, Emmanuel thought as he made notations in his book and then went over to where Phoenix stood with the mayor, looking as if he needed saving.

Thankfully the mayor's wife came along and dragged the man away. More politicking, Emmanuel thought. She was in charge of his political career. He couldn't have chosen a more worthy advocate.

"There are times his wife is a bit much, but sometimes she has perfect timing."

"Worrying about the tourists?"

"And reelection."

"Deborah says that Claudia had a computer friend that she'd planned to meet that morning. I'm going to get a subpoena for Claudia's computer."

"You do that."

"I'm out of here."

Emmanuel made his way to his car. Once there he called to the office to have the paperwork done for the subpoena, then he stopped by his house to change clothing before he returned to the office.

He had a few questions for the medical examiner.

It was after four and the fresh tracks up a dirt path were the only indication that many cars had recently traveled this isolated road. The man drove the half mile to the graveyard. It was isolated and lonely. A stranger couldn't tell that a beautiful woman was buried here today.

Still, it wasn't difficult to pick out her plot. It was the only one with a profusion of flowers.

He knew it was dangerous coming here, but he needed time alone with her. Without the husband who didn't love her. Without well-wishers and family. Without neighbors. This was his special time with her. The time they weren't allowed together when she was alive.

He parked the car in the middle of the dirt path. He still wore the black suit he'd worn to the funeral. He'd bought the suit especially for her funeral.

He didn't go into work at all today. He just couldn't. But he needed this private time to spend with her.

The baskets of flowers around her grave were a sign of many friends, the many people who loved her. All except one person—her husband. Several perfect blossoms had been picked from the basket of roses he'd had made for her. That was okay. He had more in the car. She loved roses. He wondered if many people knew of her affinity for the bloodred blossoms.

There were so many things he knew about her. He probably knew more than her own husband—like the fact that she enjoyed walking in the drizzling rain on hot days. Or that her favorite food was pork chops smothered in gravy and onions. She used to type that little smiley face when she wrote about it. She was a nurse, and she knew the fattening food wasn't good for her. But it was still her favorite.

She and Deborah had planned a trip to the museum on Saturday. She loved museums. She had planned a trip alone this summer, a week to be exact, to D.C. to just walk from one museum to the next, gazing upon art and artifacts.

He wondered if her husband knew that. He doubted it. Howard probably didn't care.

He shucked his jacket and threw it into the passenger seat. He rolled up his shirtsleeves and popped the trunk lever. He took out the shovel and the two rose bushes he'd purchased, then set them beside the grave. Then he trooped back and gathered the gallon jug of water he'd brought to water the bushes. There were baskets of flowers in the way so he moved the arrangements around the other three sides, filling in so that the arrangements looked lovely. He was meticulous with his work. When he finished, he stepped back to look at his handiwork. He'd plant the rose bushes at her head.

He briefly glanced at the sky. The sun was still bright and hot. It was like the sun was shining down on Claudia. He wiped the sweat from his face with his forearm.

Claudia would have red roses blooming through spring, summer and fall for years to come, he thought as he picked up the shovel and started to dig.

Later that afternoon, after the crowd had disappeared, Emmanuel and Gardell went to Howard's house with the warrant. Claudia's car was still parked under a tree. Howard's was in the driveway and another car was parked beside his. It wasn't the car he'd seen the other night. Emmanuel climbed from the car, walked quickly to the door, and rang the doorbell. Howard answered before he could ring it a second time.

"I hate to bother you on a day like today," Emmanuel began, "but we have a warrant to seize your wife's computer."

Howard had changed into a T-shirt and jeans. He had a beer bottle in his hand. "You didn't need to get a warrant for the computer. I'd be glad to turn it over if it'd be some help. No one wants her murderer found more than I do." He moved aside to let the men enter the house. "What do you think you'll find on the computer? I don't know anything about them. Claudia . . ." He sighed. "She was the expert."

"We appreciate your cooperation," Gardell said.

In the kitchen, platters of plastic- and foil-wrapped food were lined on the counter.

"Any reason why you want it?" Howard put his beer bottle on the table and led them to a bedroom that had been turned into a den.

"We're just checking her files for leads."

"People are saying it looks like a copycat. Like the murders between Petersburg and Richmond." He repeated what he'd told Emmanuel on his last visit.

"We're still investigating. It'll be a while—after we get the DNA results—before we can say for sure." The autopsy confirmed that her murder more than likely wasn't a copycat job, but they had sent her clothing to the FBI lab near D.C. to be evaluated by their forensics experts. It might be a while before they knew for certain, but he didn't tell Howard that.

"I guess that takes a while. Be glad when it's done. Claudia was a good woman."

Then why the hell didn't you treat her that way? Emmanuel wanted to ask, but couldn't. "She was."

"I'm sure going to miss her."

"We all will."

The computer was on a stand to the right. A little notepad was nearby. There were a couple of bookshelves with medical volumes, BET romance novels, mystery, fiction, three books by Zora Neal Hurston.

A print of the Buffalo Soldiers occupied space on one wall.

A bulletin board and calendar were attached to the wall near the desk. Emmanuel went to the calendar. It was still displaying June. His name was penciled in at eleven and there was a blank space by eleven-thirty. When he'd seen the notation before it hadn't seemed significant. She'd been dead hours before eleven-thirty. Now he thought it might be significant after all.

Emmanuel and Gardell unhooked the computer to cart it to Emmanuel's car, telling Howard good-bye.

"Y'all fix yourselves plates before you leave. There's plenty—more than I can eat."

"No, thanks," Emmanuel said. Then he went to the car with Gardell in step with him.

"Neither of us knows computers that well. You going to take it to the lab in Richmond?"

"Shari Jarrod is an expert. We'll ask Blake Industries for her help. I'll arrange for her come to the station and see what she can find."

"Smart idea. Jonathan's always willing to help."

Enlisting Shari's help satisfied two needs—assisting with the investigation, and providing him with more time with her. He tried to make himself believe that his only reason for pursuing her was that she needed him. But his budding attraction made that assessment a lie. He needed—wanted her. When she'd worn that green dress, he'd felt a pull so strong that it rocked his world from its comfortable axis. And somehow, this time, it wasn't purely about sex.

"See you at the station," he told Gardell, and then drove away.

Shari was going to discontinue her subscription to the *Nottoway Review*. Her picture with Emmanuel was plastered on the front page—again. It was the snapshot of them standing beside the limousine. Reluctantly she admired the handsome couple they made. He, strong and tall, looked very fine standing next to her. Emmanuel was too handsome for his own good. He stood several inches over her, gazing down at her instead of at the camera. Just what women loved. His hand was in the middle of her back.

She looked at the heading again and fumed. It was right beside the article featuring an update on Claudia's murder. THE DREAM DATE, it proclaimed. She hadn't seen articles on the other couples. They could have left her out and shared the page space.

"Knock, knock." Walter came into her office.

"Good morning," she said, turning the paper over. At this moment it wasn't a good morning at all.

"It's going to be, for you." He glanced at the paper but didn't mention the article.

"Why?" she asked.

"Because I just wrote the program of your dreams and tested it." He wandered to the corner where an empty chair stood and pulled it beside her desk so that they could work on the computer together. He took the keyboard in his hand.

"What program is this?"

"A new accounting program."

He demonstrated how everyone could record their own expenditures and balance them, so that she wouldn't have very much to do at the end of the month.

"You're a man after my own dreams."

"I aim to please."

"Thank you."

"Kara already has."

"Poor thing. I hated dumping it on her."

He shoved out of the chair and pushed it back to the corner. "You're a computer guru at heart, not a paper pusher."

Shari groaned. "Pushing papers is all I get to do now."

"Somebody's got to do it," he said, and left.

Shari looked after him. Walter was a wonderful human being. Very helpful, very thoughtful. He'd make some woman a wonderful husband one day. She often wondered why he hadn't found someone special by now—especially with men being as scarce as hen's teeth. She chuckled. He probably wondered the same about her.

Her eyes raked over the newspaper again. She started to trash it, then opened a drawer to get the scissors and cut out the photo. She stuffed it into her purse. Her intercom buzzed and she answered it. Jonathan's secretary summoned her to his office. She stuck the paper in the trash, locked her drawer and left for the executive corridor. Even though she was considered part of the executive staff, her office wasn't located in that area. The world over, computer rooms were stationed in the bleakest accommodations the company offered. But she couldn't complain. At Blake Industries, her window overlooked a grove of trees and flower beds in back of the building. Still, she had a long hike from her building to Jonathan's office.

The temperature was only eighty-five degrees so she wasn't sweating too much by the time she reached the main building. She marched into the rest room and used a paper towel to cool her face and pat it dry. Then she pressed a cold towel to her neck and straightened her serviceable short-sleeved jacket and slacks. After yesterday, she couldn't tolerate dark colors and long sleeves. The South was miserably hot in the summer.

She marched to Jonathan's suite. The secretary's office was larger than her own, and furnished with dark cherry furniture of understated elegance. Gorgeous valences hung from the long windows and expensive carpeting muffled her footsteps.

His secretary had been with Jonathan from the very beginning and had pretty much a free hand with things by now. Because Shari was the computer manager, she had access to all company information. She knew that the secretary could probably afford to retire but chose not to.

Right now the woman was busy reading the newspaper and glanced up at Shari. "You and Emmanuel certainly are a handsome couple," she said. "You looked nice together at the church yesterday, too."

It would do no good to tell her that she went alone and that Emmanuel had hung on to her arm and wouldn't let go, so she merely said, "Thank you," and left it at that.

"I'll buzz Jonathan for you." She did so and motioned Shari in.

Jonathan stood as she entered, and they exchanged greetings. He motioned her to the chair facing her desk. He walked around the desk and leaned against the edge.

His office was decorated similarily to his secretary's except that it was larger and more elegant. There was even a bar in the corner and he was reputed to have a private lavatory.

So did the secretary.

"Phoenix Dye called me this morning. They need help in uncovering some erased information on Claudia's computer. I've volunteered your services for it— if you're willing, during work hours."

"I'll be happy to assign someone to it," Shari said, making a note on her pad.

"They specifically requested you. The information is critical and confidential."

"But, Jonathan, there are many trustworthy people in the department. I can assign Walter. He's very experienced with computers and with the Internet. I've got so many projects on my plate."

"They desperately need help in capturing the person who murdered Claudia. I can't force you to do it, but . . ."

"Of course, I would want to help out." This was Emmanuel's doing. Shari just knew it. She wouldn't date him, so he was forcing himself on her—through his sister and her husband—with the help of the sheriff's department.

"Wonderful. You'll be on comp time until you return. Take all the time you need. Just to keep you out of public knowledge, we'll just say that I'm forcing you to take vacation time. I've noticed that you haven't taken leave this year."

Shari knew the smile on her face was stiff. "I'm sure it won't take long." She stood and they shook hands. As Jonathan turned, she noticed the paper with the picture of her and Emmanuel. Did everybody in Nottoway think she was a pitiful woman who couldn't get her own man without help?

"You can put whomever you choose in charge. It'll be up to you to update him or her."

"Walter would be the best candidate." Shari left and took the long walk back to her office. Then she beeped for Walter. He had a sickly hue to his medium brown complexion. Come to think of it, he hadn't been looking well lately.

"Are you all right, Walter?"

"Sure. Couldn't be better."

"I called you in because I'm going to be away from the office for a day or two."

Concern furrowed his brow. "Is everything all right with you and your family?"

"Yes. Jonathan's complaining that I never take time off."

"Well, that's true enough."

"Has it been that noticeable?"

"Afraid so. The people under you feel bad that they only put in nine- to ten-hour days while their boss does fourteen and fifteen."

"I certainly didn't want them to feel pressured. I have confidence in my department's abilities and performance."

Walter nodded. "That's good to hear."

"You can always reach me at my beeper number or at home." She then proceeded to go over the open projects with him.

Chapter 6

On blistering days Shari spent as much time indoors as possible. As she walked across the hot parking lot to her car, she tried to walk under as many shade trees as she could. When Shari opened the door to her Mazda, the saunalike heat rushed out to smack her in the face. She leaned inside just long enough to start the engine, then stood beside the car to wait for the heat to dissipate. Reaching inside her purse to retrieve her cell phone, she glanced at her watch. It was noon, and she still hadn't left Blake Industries.

Shari dialed the sheriff's office and asked for Emmanuel.

"Not here, ma'am. He'll be in 'round three."

Shari fumed. She hated high-handed men who went over her head to get what they wanted. With a murderer running around loose, how could he afford to take the day off?

His absence from the office didn't deter her. She knew where he lived, she thought as she stuck her head in the car to test the temperature. The worst of the heat had dispersed. She climbed in and turned the air conditioner to full blast. She'd been told that his cottage sat on the Nottoway River just a couple of miles down the road from the Riverview Restaurant and she set out in that direction, driving down Route 301 until she reached the turnoff.

The restaurant was about eight miles from Blake Industries. She soon passed the stately, tree-lined drive of the restaurant. Karina's restaurant was the best for miles. People came from as far as North Carolina and Richmond to dine there. Many cars were parked in the lot. Since several businesses had opened up in Nottoway the last few years, the Riverview was known to have a sizable lunch crowd. Shari had been warned to make reservations for that time of the day.

Shari continued down the lonely road until she reached a turnoff. It was the only turnoff past the restaurant. The dirt path to his home was so dark that one could hardly tell the day was bright and beautiful. She felt as though she was driving to some deserted spot in Mississippi. The lane was thick with trees that filtered the sunlight, and only shadows floated through the canopy.

Suddenly Shari thought of the murderer and how easy it would be to commit a murder out here in the middle of nowhere. Poor Claudia. Murdered in her own home, in her own bed, in the wee hours of the morning after her husband left for work. Shari still had trouble sleeping at night. Each little noise awakened her, and there were plenty of noises on country nights.

In a small clearing at the end of the path, the world opened up again. Bright sunshine poured down. A two-acre yard and an attractive house came into view. Behind it flowed the gentle waves of the Nottoway River.

Something was missing, Shari thought. But she couldn't quite put her finger on what. She parked her car beside Emmanuel's SUV. The songs of crickets, tree frogs, and a zillion insects were thick and soulful. An environmentalist's delight, Shari thought as she trooped to the front door. She suddenly realized what was missing.

A dog. A place like this should have a dog sprinting around the side of the house chasing a cat.

No animals came out to meet her—not a howling cat, a barking dog or anything. Outside of nature, it was quiet. The door sported a decorative brass knocker. She banged it and waited.

Birds fluttered away. Squirrels dashed through the undergrowth. Shari glanced wearily around looking for snakes that might be slithering through the grass. The place was far too isolated for her taste.

Emmanuel must be home since his car was parked in the yard. She banged the knocker a little louder. Soon she heard some rumblings from inside. The door suddenly opened.

A sleepy-eyed Emmanuel appeared wearing a hostile look. With it he wore black shorts—and nothing else. Shari glanced from his naked toes to shorts that hung midway down his thighs, then to his hairy chest, and finally to his face. In a heartbeat his expression had changed from unreceptive to welcoming. Blood raced through her body at a dizzying speed. She took a stab at composing herself, tightening her fingers around her keys until they hurt her hand.

"It's nice of you to stop by," he said, his voice low, sexy, and crowded with sleep.

His comment snapped her out of her trance. For a moment she'd forgotten why she was there. Now she hid behind her anger. "Don't play the innocent with me. You know why I'm here. You got Jonathan to release me from my job to help with the investigation. Why didn't you just ask for someone in my department, or ask me personally?"

Emmanuel shrugged, the muscles rippling in his shoulders. "You'd have said no."

Shari made an effort to look away from his body. "I would have gotten someone to work with you. Walter is the best."

"Walter isn't the manager."

"He's my assistant. And managers are best at managing—not necessarily the best with computers."

"I have it on good authority that you cut your eyeteeth on computers."

Feeling wilted as the heat poured down on her and in the absence of a rebuttal, Shari snapped, "Do I have to stand in the doorway all day?"

With a flourish Emmanuel moved to the side.

Shari looked past him as she entered his home. "Where is the computer? I want to get started right away so that I can get back to work. The sooner the better."

He rubbed the stubble on his chin. "Why don't you make yourself comfortable first?"

Suddenly she had misgivings. She thought a few

seconds and decided she was just as safe inside as outside. It wasn't as if the squirrels would come to protect her if she needed it. Then, too, she'd spent Saturday night with him—not the entire night, but on the cruise and the ride to and from Virginia Beach. And she was curious about the exquisite woodwork in the house.

She moved farther into a sizable great room. An open loft to the right loomed over the bedroom. From where she stood, she saw rumpled covers on a huge bed. The kitchen was on the left. She'd stopped a few paces from the door to look around.

"Would you like a tour?" Emmanuel asked.

Shari focused on him again, confused at her response to him, and wishing he'd put on more clothing. She hadn't felt the desire to tear off a man's clothing in all her life. The eager affection coming from him didn't help. "Perhaps after I look at the computer," she finally said, and moved to the blue-tiled counter that separated the kitchen from the great room. She set her purse and keys on the countertop. Two chairs flanked a huge comfortable navy couch. Though the woodwork was light, the furniture wasn't dainty by any measure.

"The computer isn't here. It's at the precinct."

"Oh, well, I'll go there."

"Let me give you a tour first," he said.

Shari wanted to see the house. The woodwork was impressive. "Okay. I won't stay long."

A formal dining area was next to a bay window. But the most spectacular sight was the wall of windows at the opposite side of the room, lending an unimpaired view of the Nottoway River. There were no curtains to mar the view. Beyond the windows, a deck ran the length of the house.

To the right were two closed doors. Emmanuel walked to the first door and motioned her over with a devilish smile on his face. It was a half bath with masculine striped towels. She was struck by how clean the bachelor's pad was, and she wondered if he had some woman to clean for him.

"In the next room," he said, marching toward the next door and opening it wider, "is my bedroom."

It was a huge bedroom. Larger than she would have thought in a house this size. The river side of the room had huge windows just like the other portion of the house. A queen-size bed sat in the center of the room, made of the same light wood as the cabinets.

"Did you have the bed specially made?"

"Yeah, by me."

"But it matches the kitchen cabinetry."

"I made them, too, with Jonathan and James' help."

"Are these walk-in closets?" she asked. She pointed to two closed doors across the room.

She stiffened as he marched her to the door and opened it. It was a huge master bath.

"The commode's behind that door."

"Oh, Jeez. This is lovely. What I'd give to get in a Jacuzzi like that." There was a separate shower and Jacuzzi, and two washbowls below huge mirrors.

"You're welcome any time."

Shari scoffed. "No, thank you."

"There's also a Jacuzzi out back if you'd prefer."

"Really?" She wasn't interested. She wasn't getting into a bathing suit again to sit anywhere with him. But then, visions of their swim at Virginia Beach returned. His hands on her. His arms around her. Heat suffused her body.

He was being facetious and said, "Sure." He ushered her out the room. "I'll show you."

He opened the French doors. Off to the right was a covered Jacuzzi. It was built lower than the deck, with stairs that led down to it. The top was the same level as the floor.

"Thank you for the tour. I'll let you get back to your rest."

"Have you had lunch?" he asked as he closed the door behind them.

"No, but . . ."

He rubbed his flat, washboard stomach. "Neither have I. Why don't I fix something and we'll talk while we eat?"

"Really. I have food at home."

"But you don't cook often."

"How would you know that?"

"The word is that you eat at the cafeteria at Blake Industries before you leave each evening."

"People talk too much in small towns. It must be boring if all they have to discuss is my eating habits." Between the newspaper articles and this revelation, the thought of people nosing about in her business unsettled her.

"You're the hot-shot computer person. People are bound to be interested. Plus, you bid a thousand dollars for Nottoway's most eligible bachelor."

"I *did not* bid a thousand dollars on you."

"Then how did I end up as your date?" he asked as he walked to the fridge. A smile pulled at his lips.

"You know very well how."

"I've got turkey and cheese. How about a hoagie?"

She threw up her hands. "All right. I'll make the sandwiches while you put on some clothes."

"I'm decent. But if it'll make you feel better . . ." He marched to his room.

Shari washed her hands in the half bath. He was out and donning a muscle shirt before she could dry them. The black shirt was only marginally better than the shorts.

He joined her at the fridge. She pulled out the meat and sandwich fixings while he got the rolls from a shelf, wrapped them in foil, and put them in the oven, brushing by her along the way.

"I'm dying to know why you have two full baths since you live alone and have one bedroom."

"I have two older sisters who spent hours doing God knows what in the one bathroom that we had. I was six when it started with Johanna. I'm only saying it's a good thing that we had thick private woods out back. Dad and I each had our own spots."

Shari laughed.

"Let me tell you, when you've got to go, it isn't funny."

"I know," she giggled. "I was the youngest of six."

"You had it even worse."

"We had *two* baths. Dad threatened with a belt that one bath was off-limits to hair washing, make-up donning, stockings, and long soaks. It was exclusively for, as he so eloquently put it, *what a bathroom was made to do*." She mimicked her father's tone.

When their chuckles subsided, she asked, "How long have you lived here?"

"Three years. I got builders to complete the outside and the baths and wiring inside," he said as he took the bread from the oven and plates from the cabinet.

Shari began fixing the sandwiches as they talked. "I did all the woodwork and cabinetry myself."

She looked around again. "It's gorgeous."

"Why, thank you. The next question will be why did I build it so small?"

"It had crossed my mind."

"Everybody else asks. I love my privacy."

"Oh, well, I'm sorry to intrude."

He ran the back of his hand along her face. "Not from you. I mean I can't stand a lot of people under-foot for days at a time."

"I guess that explains why you're out here in the middle of nowhere. How much land do you own?"

"A hundred acres."

"My goodness." He stood beside her. Sharp pin-pricks of sexual excitement pounded through her.

"Do . . . ahh, do you farm? Or is it just you and the trees and the river?"

"Just me," he whispered, "the trees and the river. But I'll tell you one secret. That couch in there is a queen hide-a-way." Shari stood rooted to the floor. He held her in his grip with just his velvet voice.

Finally he looked away and grabbed an unopened chip bag from the cabinet. Shari released a breath, took the bag from him with a shaky hand, and clum-sily distributed chips on both plates. He grabbed two bottles of lemonade from the fridge and directed her to the table at the bay windows.

Shari was surprised she was actually enjoying his company.

"So when do I start working on the computer?" she finally asked again. If she wanted to get out of here with her virtue intact, she'd better get down to business.

"Tomorrow."

"Why tomorrow?"

"Because I just want to talk to you today—and not about business."

"What is it?"

"Why won't you go out with me?"

Shari glanced toward the water. He looked just too sexy sitting across the table from her.

"Emmanuel, you know relationships are never serious with you."

"Maybe I'm not talking serious. Just two people getting to know each other. You know, things like dinner and a movie. Maybe play some tennis at the country club."

"I'm not a member."

"Not a problem. I am."

"The pay for detectives must be very good here."

"The club isn't elitist. Regular folks can afford memberships."

He dug into his pocket and took out some bills. "Come to the station at eight and bring dinner. I'll be back by then and you can work on the computer. The quicker you get that information, the better."

"The quicker I get to work, the quicker I finish and get back to my job."

He looked up at the ceiling. "I must have done something awful for you to get this terrible opinion you have of me." He picked up her sandwich and held it out to her.

"I just don't want to be linked with a womanizer."

"Womanizer?" He looked affronted. "I've never dated more than one woman at a time."

"But there have been *so many* of them."

"Not that many." He moved the sandwich to her lips.

She tried to move away, then bit into it and began to chew. He moved his finger across her lips, and Shari kissed the finger that lingered there in the long silence.

Embarrassed at what she'd done, Shari glanced out the window again, trying for distance. "How can you stand having your windows open all the time?"

"Would you feel better if I had blinds?"

"I don't live here, but I'd think you'd want privacy at night."

He marched to the countertop, picked up a remote control, and pushed something. She heard a rumble and a hidden compartment over the windows opened up to expose blinds that slowly lowered. In seconds, the windows were completely covered.

"Feel better?"

"Much. But you can leave them open now."

He opened them and the gorgeous view once again presented itself. After he put the remote on the bar, he gently pulled Shari from the chair.

Desire had ridden her so high that she stood on shaky legs, leaning toward him.

"I want to kiss you," he said.

"What are you waiting for?" she asked, aware that she was weaving back and forth. Wanting, yet afraid to want.

He leaned down and put his mouth to hers. Their bodies pressed into each other, her soft breasts compressed against his chest.

They kissed deeply, as if they'd waited a lifetime for this moment.

Emmanuel felt her hands hesitate on his back as

his tongue dueled with hers. He savored every inch of her mouth. He inched his hand across the curve of her backside, holding her close to him. He ground his hips against her. He'd never felt this deep abiding attraction before, as if he had to have her—or else. He flicked his tongue around her mouth, tiny back and forth movements that drove him wild.

Before he could stop himself, he'd lifted Shari into his arms and carried her to the couch, their mouths still pressed together. He gently laid her on the cushions and lowered his body to hers. He trailed kisses down her slim, soft neck. He moved his hips against hers, then trailed kisses along her collarbone. He undid the top buttons of her jacket and stroked her breasts.

He was surprised to find front fasteners on her bra—so unlike the plain picture she presented to the world. He released the fastening and her soft breast spilled out into his hand. He stroked and caressed and moved his mouth to suckle gently on her nipple. Her moans stirred his desire to a fever pitch and sent hot licks of fire coursing through his body as he moved back to her mouth and kissed her hard, sliding his hands down to her hips. Pressing his body urgently against hers, he grasped both her hands in his and held them above her head as he moved in a sensual dance against her.

She moved against him, her movements driving him crazy. He kissed her deeper. She pulled against him, her hips rolling and bucking. Suddenly her struggle broke through his frenzied haze, and he realized she was fighting him. Emmanuel immediately released her.

What he saw frightened him. Stark terror shone on her face. He got up quickly.

"What's wrong?" he asked.

She gulped deep breaths and sat up suddenly, backing from him to the corner of the couch.

"Shari?" he said, afraid to approach her. "It's okay. I won't do anything to you."

"You . . . you."

"I'm not going to hurt you." How could he have forgotten that there were secrets beneath her façade? He reached out to her. She drew back. "It's okay. I just want to comfort you."

Her expression kept him at a distance. He handed her a pillow. She took it and curled her arms around it. He didn't want to leave her, but he got up, went to the kitchen, and poured her a glass of ice water. Covertly he watched her. She hovered in the corner of the couch, hugging the pillow for dear life.

She took the glass from him and held it in her hand.

Emmanuel sat at the other end of sofa talking to her softly, saying anything he thought would soothe her.

Finally she sipped at the cold water and held the glass against her forehead.

"You want to tell me about it?" Emmanuel asked again.

She trembled, but was still unable to move.

"Shari, may I hold you? I won't do anything. Just hold you."

After a moment, she nodded.

Slowly he moved closer to her and gathered her in his arms. She leaned stiffly against him. He stroked her arm softly as he continued to talk, simple, meaningless words, designed to soothe her. She remained silent, but whatever he said must have been working because by slow degrees she began to relax.

Minutes passed before he pressed again, first lifting her hand in his and kissing her knuckle. "Can you talk to me about what happened? About what I did to upset you?"

She inhaled a deep breath. "I thought I was over it."

"Over what?" he asked. But the moment was shattered by the ringing phone. Emmanuel ignored it. It continued to ring until the answering machine clicked on.

"Emmanuel! If you're there, pick up." It was Phoenix Dye.

"I have to get that," Emmanuel said, and gently left her. He answered the phone, still watching Shari.

Another body had been found—in Chesterfield— this time with indications that it was the work of the serial killer.

He swore. Right now was the worst possible time to leave Shari. He wanted to stay with her until he'd heard her entire story. He wanted to help her through this crisis, but she seemed much more composed by the time he disconnected.

She'd left the seat to retrieve her purse and keys from the countertop and was on her way to the door.

Emmanuel caught up with her before she opened it. "We need to talk about this, Shari."

"I know," she said, "but not right now."

He grabbed his keys and followed her outside. "Will you bring my dinner tonight? To the station?"

She nodded her head.

"I'll drive you home."

"No, I'm okay." She looked as if she were embarrassed by her actions.

Emmanuel wanted her to trust him. "Are you sure you're okay? I won't leave if you're not."

She tried to smile. "It wasn't you. I'm okay. Really."

He stroked her hair tenderly. "I'll see you tonight?"

She nodded, and climbed into her car.

Emmanuel went to the SUV and followed her home. As soon as she shut the door behind her, he left.

When Emmanuel returned home, he dressed quickly and drove toward Chesterfield.

On the way he got word that the autopsy on the last strangling victim was being done in Richmond late that afternoon. I-95 was busy during the summer with so many tourists traveling north and south for summer vacations. On the weekend all the hotels near the main road from Washington to South Carolina would be filled. Johanna's hotel never had a spare room during the summer.

On his drive Emmanuel thought of Shari. He realized he was probably wearing on her somewhat, hoped she was beginning to trust him.

First he'd drive to Chesterfield, then on to Richmond to the autopsy. Autopsies were tough scenes to view. Many policemen didn't like to attend them and Emmanuel was no exception. Most bailed after only a few minutes. It reminded him of TV's Quincy who used the autopsy trick whenever he wanted to get on with more pressing business. Within minutes, the class had either left or they were laid out on the floor.

Attending this autopsy got him down to the raw basis of human form, but it was also the quickest means to information. Otherwise, he'd have to wait days, maybe weeks, to get a copy of the official autopsy report.

The victim was a woman about two years older than Claudia. And just like Claudia, she'd been strangled. Her hands and feet had been bound with athletic tape. She'd been raped and left in the woods off Route 301. The murder had occurred around six A.M. The rapist had used a prophylactic, but unlike Claudia's case, he'd left a calling card. And this the police had kept from the media just as they had Claudia's asphyxiation with the use of a pillow.

The killer had left a red carnation in the woman's hand—a bloodred carnation that could be found in any supermarket around town.

A copycat wouldn't have known to do that.

Chapter 7

Emmanuel made it back to the station by five-thirty. The smell of the autopsy was in his hair, in his sinuses, in his clothing. He quickly headed to the shower. Emmanuel used lemon shampoo and shower gel to get rid of the scent. Cleaning the scent from his body was easy enough to do, but wiping Shari's terror from his mind proved impossible. He'd worried about her all afternoon. It had been wrenching to leave her today.

He planned to check on her to make sure she was okay. God, what had someone done to her? He wanted to hunt the person down and tear them apart with his bare hands. He'd tried to reach her from his cell phone on his way from Chesterfield, but she didn't answer. He didn't know if she was sitting home alone or if she'd visited her sister or brother. He only hoped she wasn't alone.

Emmanuel turned the shower off and tucked the towel around his waist. He gathered his clothing in the tiny locker room. A couple of guys had come in to change.

"Hey, Emmanuel," Joe said. "Heard you were making time with that computer lady that bid a fortune on you." Joe was one of the older men on the force— about fifty-two. There had been resentment between the two men since Phoenix had promoted Emmanuel to the detective slot. Those positions didn't come around often, and Joe didn't understand that he wasn't chosen because he was known to put in the least amount of effort for the job. Criminals weren't lax; neither could a detective afford to be.

Emmanuel tugged on his pants, ignoring the man.

But Joe wasn't fazed by his silence. "Now, I want you to tell me something." He sat on the other end of the bench and pulled off his smelly sneakers. "With her making all that money, how're you gonna wear the pants?"

Emmanuel plucked his shirt off the chair and leaned close to Joe, shoving one arm through the armhole. "I don't have a problem with that, Joe. But I hear if I run into problems I can get advice from you."

That got a loud guffaw from the other officer who'd come in with Joe and he twisted his mouth into a smile that didn't quite reach to his eyes and stomped into his other shoe.

Emmanuel left the locker room for his office. Joe's comment gave him pause. He'd never thought that much about having a lot of money. Johanna was the miser in the family—counting her pennies and nickels from the time she learned her numbers. Since he'd completed the carpentry on the inside of his house, it was paid for. He had no outstanding debts, and as long as a decent roof covered his head, food filled his stomach, he had enough cash to entertain dates and a bit put aside for a rainy day, money didn't concern him that much. He led a very simple life and he enjoyed his work. What more could a man want—besides a good woman?

Women were different, however. As head of a computer department, Shari's salary probably more than doubled a county detective's. The fact that he made so much less might concern her.

And for that reason, it began to nag at him, even though he realized he was rushing her—and himself.

"Tonight isn't a good night for dinner," Shari told her brother Gerald who'd invited her out. She gazed out the window, holding the portable phone to her ear. Karl's yellow Mustang pulled into the lane across the road from her. He and his family lived down the long driveway.

"I haven't seen you for some time. Everything okay?" he asked.

"Just fine." Soft music played in the background.

"You don't sound it."

Shari tensed. "But I am," she said. "Are you free tomorrow?"

The sound of him flipping pages in his Day-Timer came clearly through the wire.

"Yes," he finally said.

Shari left the window and pulled open the freezer. "I'll fix dinner for you." A trip to the supermarket was called for.

"I never turn down a home-cooked meal. How did the date in Norfolk go?"

"Very well. We stayed on the beach and went swimming the next morning."

"You're not getting serious about Emmanuel, are you?"

"Are you getting serious about anyone?" she asked, annoyed. Gerald didn't want her dating Emmanuel while Clarice thought he was the best thing since sliced bread.

"We're talking about you. Emmanuel's . . ."

She bristled at his interference. "Stop it right there. I don't want to hear another word."

Silence greeted her. "I'll see you tomorrow." The statement was issued like a command. Shari didn't take commands.

"Not to grill me on Emmanuel."

Shari slowly pushed the off button on her cordless phone and closed the freezer door then ran a hand over her face. She'd debated all afternoon whether she should meet Emmanuel at the station as he'd requested.

She remembered the last time she'd tried intimacy. It occurred a couple of months after the attack. She had been dating her boyfriend, Steven, for a year, and he was fed up with waiting for her to recover. The experience had been a nightmare. Intimacy had frightened her. He'd tried to console her in his own fashion. He patted her on the hand but made a hasty exit afterward. *Maybe next time it won't be so bad,* he'd said on his way out the door.

They'd tried again a week later. Shari had been apprehensive about trying so soon after the first episode. That second time was even worse. Stephen hopped up and snapped, *I can't take you freaking out on me like I'm some animal. What happened is over. You've got to get on with your life, else I'm getting on with mine.*

She'd tried to get on with her life, but not to his satisfaction. He got on with his life. Shari got on with hers, too, such as it was. Months passed before she realized they had attempted intimacy far too soon. Mentally she hadn't healed.

Shari tried to think about what caused the relapse this time. She had been enjoying Emmanuel's love-making, his scent, the texture of his hands sliding over her body. His taste. Her desire had built to a fever pitch. She didn't fear him, but suddenly she couldn't move, and her helplessness immediately threw her back to that awful night.

Emmanuel hadn't been disgusted. He hadn't been impatient. He'd been caring and solicitous. It was nice to be held afterward. In the past she'd always suffered alone. As she left his house, she'd been shocked to look through her rearview mirror and see his SUV following her home. It touched a place in her heart to know that he cared that much.

Now he'd had time to think about her reaction, and Shari was leery of what his response would be. She wasn't afraid, or even embarrassed, because she knew that the rape that had torn her life apart hadn't been her doing. She had no reason to be ashamed. Still, Emmanuel was the kind of man accustomed to getting what he wanted, when he wanted it. Waiting was foreign. His compassion may not extend to accepting a woman with a history. Steven's certainly hadn't.

Right now she debated whether she should meet

him for dinner or beg off. If she postponed it, dating again would be so much more difficult the next time.

Shari had never run from life in the past. She met it head-on. It was time that she recovered the courage that had been snatched away by that one awful incident. She'd face Emmanuel, and if he had second thoughts about her now that he knew her secret, then so be it. She wasn't running.

Shari ran upstairs and showered, tucked the towel around her, and searched for something to wear. All her clothing was baggy and unattractive. Tonight she wanted to wear something sharp. She continued to look until she stopped at a pair of jeans Clarice had given her ages ago, saying that she'd brought them from mail order but the sizes ran small and they should fit Shari. Shari guessed her sister was trying to subtly give her hints. It hadn't worked because Shari had thrown them to the back of her closet and forgotten about them.

Now she donned the tight jeans and a flowing aqua top. The aqua brought out the liveliness of her skin tone. Thank goodness the top covered her hips, she thought as she posed in front of the mirror.

Before she could stop herself, she picked up the phone and called in an order at Karina's for two dinners to go. Then she dabbed on a light-scented cologne. Before she chickened out, she grabbed her purse and left.

When she arrived at the restaurant, it was packed and she was glad that she'd ordered ahead. And as soon as she walked into the foyer, she saw her brother. He stood by the table that displayed a sculpture by their local artist, Patrick, whose work was sought after nationally.

"I thought you were busy tonight," Gerald said. Evidently he hadn't made a reservation and now waited for a table.

"I am," she said, and let the hostess know she was there to pick up an order.

"Who's the second dinner for?" Gerald asked when the hostess left to get it.

"None of your business."

He perused her outfit. "You're looking different."

Shari smiled. "Who are you here with?"

"Towanna."

Her dinners arrived, and she paid. "I'll see you tomorrow."

"Definitely," he said, watching her as she left.

On the drive to the sheriff's office, she was apprehensive but she arrived precisely at eight. Several cars were parked in the lot and when she walked into the building, the mayor had cornered Phoenix by his door. The light had been turned off in his office and the secretary had gone. She didn't have a clue where to find Emmanuel. Other than the two men, the place looked deserted.

Emmanuel had driven by Shari's on his way from an interview for another case, but she'd left. He glanced at the cars parked in front of the station and smiled.

"Sorry I'm late," he said when he entered the building in a rush and spotted her.

"I just arrived."

Emmanuel sniffed the air and said, "Oh, good. Dinner." He lifted the bag from her arms, grasped her hand, and marched her upstairs, through the large squad room and to his office. He stopped long enough to unlock and open his door. Several offices surrounded the squad room. They were all closed.

It was a utilitarian office, about half the size of hers, with a couple of modern file cabinets pushed back against one wall and a huge whiteboard with diagrams and cases scribbled on it. A stack of folders and a computer sat on his desk.

"Where's the computer?" she asked.

"In the evidence room." He rummaged in the bag. "Let's eat first, then I'll take you there."

She watched him closely as he glanced in the boxes. "They're both stuffed pork chops. 'The other white meat.' I hope you eat pork."

"A woman after my own heart. I'll eat anything from Karina's." He handed her a plate with such a heated look, she took a step back. Then he pointed to the chair beside his desk. Slowly she approached the chair and sat down. He had already dug into his food as if he hadn't just eaten a few hours before. She guessed that with his height and build, he needed extra fuel.

"What are you waiting for?" he finally asked.

Shari smiled and unfastened the top of her box.

"You look very pretty tonight," he said.

Shari glanced at him, apprehensive. "Thank you." She picked up her fork, then on a deep sigh she put it down. "About today . . ."

Emmanuel put down his fork and shoved his plate back. He got up and closed the door. Then he came back and swiveled his chair so that he and Shari faced each other. They were so close, their knees touched. Gently he took both her trembling hands and kissed her knuckles.

"Tell me about it," he said softly.

Silence rang in the air. Could she trust him? She searched his eyes. Concern clearly showed on his face. He'd been kind to her on their date together. And she couldn't stay away from men forever. Perhaps with the problems he'd had to deal with on his job, he would be more sensitive and understand the emotional turmoil that she suffered and continued to endure. She'd only talked with her psychologist and her women's group about this, but she couldn't run away from it any longer.

She cleared her throat. "It happened two and a half years ago."

"What happened?" he asked softly.

"After work, I went to a bar with a coworker. We'd worked late that Friday night. It was around nine when we left. The bar served buffalo wings and celery sticks dipped in blue cheese dressing." She laughed. "I loved their recipe. We had appetizers over a glass of wine. We talked about the software we were developing and the problems we were running into. Time passed quickly and I barely touched my wine. I thought that finally, after fighting me for so long, he'd be willing to work companionably with me on this project. Anyway, two hours later, I went to the ladies' room. When I returned, I continued to sip my drink. Before I knew it, I felt really dizzy." She stopped talking. She didn't realize tears were running down her face.

Emmanuel wanted to hold her in his arms, but knew she wouldn't accept his comfort just yet. He held her hands to give her support, and he forced himself to stay in his seat. He could barely stand it.

"What do you remember next?" he rasped. His throat was clogged with emotion.

Shari's hand balled into a fist beneath his. "I remembered waking up in his bed. It must have been just after he'd finished. I remember the smell of the sweat on his skin mixed with his cologne. I remember the mirror above his bed. In the low light I watched his body on mine, and I couldn't push him off."

"The Rohypnol?"

She nodded. Anger burned in the pit of Emmanuel's stomach, but he stifled his emotions to deal with hers.

"What do you remember next?" he asked.

"I was so groggy, the next thing I remember was waking in my own bed."

He rubbed her hand. "Did you report him?"

She nodded. "It all seemed like a dream, so it was a while before I realized what happened. But he'd used a prophylactic. He told the police that I was drunk and he drove me home. The waitress said that I'd only had one drink, but it seemed to her that I needed assistance when I left. She thought that people who weren't drinkers had more of a reaction to alcohol. The only thing the doctor could tell was that I'd had sex. There wasn't any DNA for him."

Emmanuel knew she had brothers and a father. He was sure they'd have dealt with the situation, but to be certain, he asked. "Did you tell your family?"

She shook her head.

He frowned. "Why not?"

"Because I wanted to handle it on my own. Even at thirty, I'm considered the baby of the family. I didn't want my family taking care of things for me, and I didn't want them to worry. I took care of it."

"How?"

"I used the Web. There are ways to send messages without your user ID, so I sent an internal mail message that he was a rapist. He blamed me, but there was no proof. Come to find out, I wasn't the only woman this had happened to. He'd threatened them. That fool acted as though he hadn't done anything wrong."

"Who is he?" Emmanuel asked.

"Who *was* he? He was married. Can you believe that? He died a month after that in a car accident. I wanted him to go to trial for what he did. I didn't want him to die. Death was too easy. All the women he'd raped were getting together with a team of lawyers to bring him to trial. We couldn't take a dead man to trial."

"If he was married, how did he take you home?"

"When his wife and children visited her parents, he found ways to rape women. I wanted to put black roses on his coffin, but I couldn't. I couldn't hurt his children or his wife. She was as much a victim as we were."

"Have you had counseling?" He realized that she probably had, especially since she was the brains behind the Women's Center.

"I was in therapy for a year. I thought I was doing pretty well until . . . well."

"What happened?"

"My boyfriend couldn't be bothered with a repressed woman. There were too many who were ready and willing and without baggage from the past."

"The son of a . . ." Anger boiled over in Emmanuel in the face of such insensitivity. He caressed her face gently, wishing he could absorb some of her pain. It wasn't enough that she'd been raped. Some insensitive fool couldn't keep it in his britches long enough to deal with her crisis.

"He wasn't the right one for you," he said fiercely. "You're better off without him. I'll bet he'll be traveling from woman to woman for the rest of his life, never finding a true meaningful relationship because he isn't willing to nurture it. You're better off waiting for the right man. And I'm that man, Shari." Emmanuel almost wondered if he was talking about his own former existence. He'd roamed from woman to woman, but he hoped he wasn't as callous as that.

Emmanuel's face was so close to Shari that she reached out and touched his cheek with her hand. "You certainly aren't a for-keeps man."

"I can be," he whispered, and for the first time, Emmanuel meant what he said. He did want someone he could settle with. He wanted to help her get over her past. He leaned toward her and pressed his mouth to hers for a brief kiss of comfort. "Give me a chance," he whispered against her lips.

She smiled and ran her tongue over her lips. "I think . . . we'll see. Thanks for listening."

"We'll start with a movie Friday night. Let me show you that men can be trusted. Let me help you live again."

Shari glanced down at her hand. "We'll see," she repeated.

Emmanuel smiled. "I can live with that."

Emmanuel's phone rang. He scooted his chair back, picked up the receiver, and listened.

"I'll be down in a few minutes." He hung up and

asked Shari, "Do you want a crack at the computer while I'm gone?"

"That's what I'm here for," she replied. "Do you have any clues yet?"

"Well, her pen pal's screen name has been erased, so we can't get the identity from the Internet provider. Why don't you eat first? I'll get the computer from the evidence room and roll it in here."

"Sounds good. Suddenly I'm starved." She opened the box, forked some of the delicious stuffing into her mouth, and sighed in pleasure. Who needed to cook when Karina's offered such delicious meals?

"How late are you working tonight?" she asked.

"Until midnight."

"I should have something to tell you before then."

He watched her silently for a few moments, and she was uneasy under his close scrutiny. Then he left, and Shari was alone in the office with the computer and her thoughts.

At a quarter to twelve, Emmanuel came to check on her. "Did you find anything?" he asked. Her eyes were slightly red. She'd woken early today. While she worked on the computer, other officers stopped by to talk. She discovered that Emmanuel had worked most of the night before.

"I certainly did. I uncovered the screen name 'T_Byte.' With the last name being Byte I would imagine he's a computer person. She had a conversation with him the night before she was killed. The message reads like they'd made the date about a week before Claudia was murdered."

"You came up with a lot of information in just a couple of hours."

"I worked in computer security at my last job. With the right software"—she held up a CD—"you can read just about any file, even erased files, on a PC." She handed him several sheets of printouts.

"That's it?"

"That's it."

He scanned the sheets. "We'll get a warrant tomorrow for the Internet provider to get this person's name, address, and phone number."

Shari shut down the computer and waited as Emmanuel returned the computer to the property room and put her findings in the file on Claudia. Then he left a message for Phoenix. Shari's information narrowed the playing field to two men—her husband, who could have known that Claudia was meeting her computer date, and the computer date himself. The answer lay in the motive and opportunity. He still wasn't sure that her husband couldn't have committed the murder. And why would her computer date murder her? Unless he was the sort of man who'd done it before. There might be another serial killer right under his nose.

Chapter 8

Emmanuel walked Shari to her car. "I'll follow you home and make sure you get in okay," he said, trying to be casual.

"You don't have to do that."

"Humor me."

He closed her car door and walked to his own vehicle. After he followed her home, he went inside with her. She looked sloe-eyed and sexy.

"It's good that you get to take tomorrow off," he said once they were in her house.

"I'll probably go in around nine. Since I'm finished with the project. Will you go in at three?"

"No. I have to be at the office early to get the warrant and contact the Internet provider."

"I see. Well then, I guess it's bedtime for both of us."

That was a loaded statement if he ever heard one.

"Is it okay if I kiss you again?" He walked close to her and took her hands in his before she could stop him. "Or," he said with a slow smile, "you can kiss me."

Shari smiled. "You don't give up, do you?"

"Never," he said, and pulled her close. He put his arms around her. As he tilted her chin, he could see the uncertainty gathering in her eyes—could feel the staccato beat of her heart against his chest. For a moment he merely held her loosely in his arms and watched her. Then he lowered his head, kissed her cheek, and rubbed her back seductively. He pressed her head against his chest and continued to stroke her. Then he kissed her forehead with a feather-light touch and stepped away.

"I'll see you Friday," he said, and strolled to the door. He let himself out into the warm night. The stars were shining bright and clear. Not a cloud was in sight. But his system was boiling over with need. Denial built character, his father had always told him. He guessed his character would grow stronger than ever in the weeks ahead.

Shari stood in the middle of the room and touched her hand to her cheek. Her heart hammered in her chest as hard as if she'd run five miles. Excitement and desire rushed through her. Not the fear she'd anticipated after yesterday's fiasco. Was what she felt real? Had his words been real? Or did she believe him because she needed so much to be able to trust again?

* * *

Emmanuel knew he should drive straight home to sleep, but he also knew that with Shari on his mind he wouldn't sleep a wink for hours. Instead of heading toward home, he drove to downtown Nottoway.

Route 301 ran parallel to Interstate 95 and he chose that because I-95 was wall-to-wall trucks this time of night. When he finally made it downtown, it was quiet. Only streetlights shone in the night. The one exception was the light from the front of a lone bar with several pickups and cars parked outside. One of them was a sunshine-yellow Mustang. Jukebox music blared from inside.

Emmanuel left the car and entered the dimly lit room. Game machines pinged from an adjacent room off to the side. Several people, mostly men, sat around nursing beer or liquor. The man whom Emmanuel had seen with Jonathan at the graveyard sat at a small table in the corner nursing a drink.

Emmanuel went to the bar, ordered a beer, and took the bottle to the game room. He lounged at the door watching Gardell play pool with Karlton. At the pinball machine Karl was making out with Darla who was two years older than he. The kid pressed in close behind her and guided her hands—as if she really needed help playing pinball. The other hand slid to the tight green skirt that barely covered her behind and up her thigh to her hip. Emmanuel shook his head. The boy's hormones were raging pure sex. Darla seemed to be enjoying the byplay.

Karlton took a sip of something while he waited for Gardell to take his shot.

"I hope that's soda," Emmanuel said, straightening in the doorjamb.

"What else?" Karlton put his glass on the table when Gardell missed.

Gardell stifled a curse.

"Show time," Karlton said, eyed the remaining balls, then bent over the table.

"What're you doing up so late?" he said to Gardell.

"Couldn't sleep." Gardell broke the balls.

"Same here." Gardell had a lot to live down—his father's reputation and subsequent death while he served out his sentence. A father was still a father regardless of what he'd done. It must have been tough for Gardell to return to Nottoway. But Nottoway was home and there wasn't a place on earth like home.

The next morning, Emmanuel was exhausted. The comment Joe made yesterday about Shari's salary kept him up late. He could deal with earning less than Shari. Still he wasn't quite sure what he felt about that. His mom never worked outside the home. If he ever found someone with whom he could make a true partnership, he didn't think the money would bother him. He wanted to feel that he'd be contributing his share. He filled his cup with coffee and stepped outside. The heat had climbed to eighty, and it was only seven-thirty.

He didn't know his net worth, but his sister Johanna knew. She was the family's investment counselor, not necessarily by choice. He climbed into the SUV and left for her place. On his way, he passed the Nottoway Inn, his sister's hotel. The stately building that had hosted a legion of famous musicians in the twenties and thirties was surrounded by well-manicured lawns.

Johanna and Jonathan's home was just down the road from the hotel. He drove into the yard of a house built in the 1700s and walked to the back door. The heart of the house was on the ground level, leaving the upstairs for more formal entertaining.

In houses this old, the kitchen was originally built in a separate building, but one had been built on the ground level in the 1950s.

A white apron covered Jonathan's dress shirt and suit pants. He was dishing food at the table and the twins were sitting down to breakfast.

Emmanuel shook his head. Marriage hadn't domesticated his sister. As for the twins, he still found it difficult to believe that Johanna had children. She didn't appear to be the motherly type. Actually, she was a very protective and loving mother; she just wasn't one to make home-cooked meals and spend her mornings cleaning like their mom did.

"Grab a chair, Emmanuel," Jonathan said, "and eat with us."

"No, thanks," Emmanuel replied. He was holding out hope that Shari would soon share breakfast with him.

"So, how's the search going with Shari?"

"Already done," he said. "Found everything by midnight. She'll be back at work this morning."

Jonathan put a pan in the sink. "She should take the day off. I'm going to have to force her to take a vacation."

Emmanuel smiled. "That works for me."

"So that's the way the wind blows."

"Which way is it blowing, Dad?" Trance asked.

"We'll see when we go outside. We'll check the weather vane."

Johanna strolled in, inserting a ruby earring in her ear. "Hi, Emmanuel. What brings you here?" She wore a navy power suit with a mauve blouse.

"I can't visit my niece and nephew?"

"On a workday morning?"

"Before I forget"—Jonathan cut in—"can you pick up the children from day care today?"

She tugged at his tie, bringing his face close to hers for a kiss. "It's going to cost you," she whispered against his lips.

Jonathan gathered her into his arms for a kiss then let her go to fill her cup with coffee.

Little Terri puckered up her forehead. "How come you're charging Dad, Mom?"

"Because, sweetheart, nothing in life is free."

"What're you going to charge him?" the little girl wanted to know.

Johanna put a finger to her chin. "I've got to think about it." She went to the stove, dished up a plate of food, and sat at the table.

Emmanuel shook his head. "She's a pistol."

"You can say that again." Trance rolled his eyes toward the ceiling—eyes that were too knowledgeable for a five-year-old.

"How about this?" Jonathan said, and swooped down and kissed his wife solidly.

"There they go again," the twins said in unison, and proceeded to eat their breakfast. But Terri put down her fork and watched her parents. When they parted, she asked, "What're you going to charge him for the kiss, Mom? I bet it's gonna be a whole lot."

Johanna inhaled on a pleased sigh. "Not a cent, darling."

Terri puckered up her forehead again. "Why not?"

"Because," Johanna said, leaning toward her daughter with a secret smile on her face, "your daddy's kisses are priceless."

Terri bounced in her seat. "I want one too, Daddy."

Jonathan plucked her out of the chair, gave her a big hug and a kiss on the cheek, and nuzzled her neck. She giggled.

Emmanuel looked on with a wistful sigh. He envied the comfort, the love this family demonstrated. Jonathan was the perfect man for his sister. Though he was extremely wealthy and the largest business owner in the town or any town within fifty miles, his heart was even bigger. He had drive and ambition to more than match Johanna's, but not so that he lost sight of the real values in life. It wasn't the money that made the difference. In Jonathan's case, he'd had to raise his fourteen-year-old sister when their parents died during his first year of graduate work. He'd immediately left college to return home and started the small business of his dreams. Now that business had grown to have several thousand employees.

Johanna owned the town's only hotel. Eight years ago she'd refurbished the classic Art Deco structure, built in the 1920s just a few years before the stock market crash.

Emmanuel has always wanted to be a detective. Shari had enormous drive just like Johanna. He wondered if she'd think he was lacking somehow. Would she eventually feel they weren't a good fit?

"Okay, kids, kiss Mom good-bye and grab your backpacks. Time to go," Jonathan said.

The twins ran over to their mom for hugs and then toward the door. "Bye, Uncle E."

"See you later," he replied.

"When do we get to stay at your house again?"

Emmanuel stifled a groan. "Soon," he said, and left it at that. They grabbed the backpacks by the door and stormed out the house. Jonathan grabbed his suit jacket off the chair, his briefcase from the door, and followed them, first pausing long enough to kiss his wife.

"Sure you aren't going to join me for breakfast?" Johanna asked, sipping her coffee after they left.

He shook his head and reached for the coffee and poured himself a cup. He tasted it and sighed. Jonathan had made the coffee. Johanna still couldn't make it fit to drink. What would this family do without the man?

"So what brings you here?"

He held the cup in both hands and prepared himself for the knowing look he'd get from her once he asked about his money. He'd never consulted her before. He knew that once he needed it, the money would be available. Johanna was a woman to be trusted. He was well aware that you couldn't turn money over to just anybody and expect it to be there and not embezzled. Johanna was always meticulous and trustworthy.

"I was wondering what I'm worth. Financially." Since Emmanuel's very first paycheck, Johanna had invested a portion for the future. It all started when he was five and she was twelve and their dad had given him four quarters. She'd sat on the steps with him while he'd waited for Dad to take him to the store for a Popsicle. She explained that as long as he lived with Mom and Dad, he should save half his money. But he didn't want to save half. He had enough money for a Popsicle and candy. Then she tried to snatch two quarters from him, resulting in a tug-of-war. He screamed, punched and kicked her.

The noise brought their mom tearing out the house demanding to know what she'd done to him. Johanna had screamed at him that he was going to wind up a beggar on the streets because he didn't save any money. He'd wanted that candy so badly, his mouth watered. She foretold a dismal future in graphic detail. The fact that he wouldn't have a roof over his head, no family, and no food scared him so badly, he'd thrown two quarters at her and had done without his candy. Since that day, Johanna had handled his investments. Johanna was too young to open an account at a brokerage house and their parents knew nothing about stocks, so Smith, the previous owner of the Nottoway Inn, handled the transactions for Johanna once she decided on a stock. Most, however, were through dividend investment plans. Once a share was purchased, it was only a matter of mailing payments. When he'd started a paper route at eleven, she'd taken seventy-five percent, saying that was too much money for him to waste. They'd fought about that, too.

"What brings this on?"

"It's time I knew."

Her smile was too smug for Emmanuel's comfort. "It's about time. But I think it has more to do with masculine pride. What is it? Do you think Shari won't accept you because you don't make as much money as she does?''

She'd hit it on the nail.

"No. Of course not." He covered his reaction by lifting his cup to his lips.

Johanna gave him a knowing look. "You have about six hundred thousand."

The cup dropped to the table. The coffee remaining in it splattered on the surface. Emmanuel was speechless. Then he tightened his mouth and righted the cup, taking napkins from the holder to blot up the spill. "Don't play games, Johanna."

"I'm not. In a couple of years you'll have close to a million. I've been investing your money in stocks since you were six. I'd wait until I collected enough for a share or two and just keep adding on. You've been saving for twenty-five years. And you made pretty good money on your paper routes. Over the last twenty years, the market has skyrocketed. Now you make far more off your investments than your salary," she said. "So"—she leaned closer to him for effect—"you don't have to feel inferior to Shari. Financially you're probably her equal."

Emmanuel didn't know whether to be angry or glad. "You're a piece of work, you know that? I could have afforded to hire a builder for my house and not work myself to the bone on my time off."

"True. But you can't tell the difference. You did a fabulous job on that house. And it was a great personal experience. My husband and James needed that masculine outlet on Saturday mornings."

Emmanuel frowned. He simply couldn't digest the fact that he had so much money at thirty. His miserly sister had really come through for him this time.

Johanna narrowed her eyes. "And don't get any ideas about spending any of it."

"What am I supposed to do? Die with all that money stashed away?"

"When you really need it, it'll be there."

The truth was, he had everything he needed. Still, when he'd mentioned once that maybe he should stop the saving so that he could have more money for his house, Johanna had him thinking he was so poor, that he'd barely got by. She had pitched such a fit, he'd told her to forget it. How he hated fighting with women. The house was the size he wanted it, but he'd had to scrimp to get that. He'd used trees from his own land to build the cabinets. He'd hopped all over the place making deals so he could afford materials. At night he'd fallen into bed so tired he could barely move, muscles so sore they screamed.

And all the while his sister was hording every stinking cent.

"If you weren't my sister, I could really hate you."

"And why?" she asked self-righteously. Only Johanna could miss the point.

Emmanuel noted her indignant expression and knew she'd never understand. Johanna was Johanna. Suffer now for a better tomorrow.

"You'd never understand," he said, standing. "Gotta go."

"Hold on a minute. You didn't tell me how things are with you and Shari."

"Mind your business. You're in too much of mine already," he said, and left with her irritating chuckles following him.

Emmanuel drove toward Shari's place. She should be up by now, and if not . . . well that was okay, too.

But Emmanuel didn't get to go to Shari's. He got a call that another serial killing victim had been found—in Chesterfield. He dropped by the office long enough to give Phoenix info for the computer subpoena to be assigned to someone to get the warrant, and he was off. Interstate 95 and he were becoming good buddies, he thought as he sped north. Rush-hour traffic was steady, but he'd seen rush hour at the Mixing Bowl close to D.C. and wouldn't complain. As he drove, his mind turned to Shari. He picked up his cell phone and dialed her number, wondering if he'd catch her sleepy voice. She answered on the second ring.

"Did I wake you?"

"I've been up for an hour; I'm on my second cup of coffee."

"Damn." He would have liked to sit across from her and sip on her to his pleasure, along with that coffee.

"If I get back in time, how about dinner?"

"You said Friday."

"Can't wait that long."

She laughed. "You're something else. Sure, but Gerald and Clarice are coming over. Tylan's out of town and the children are spending the week with his sister."

"The more the merrier." He'd really like to have her to himself, but in lieu of that, seeing her with a crowd was better than not at all.

He hung up. Just hearing her voice made his day better.

Forty-five minutes later, he arrived at the scene of the crime. Officers had cordoned off the area and the investigative team was already on the job.

There were similarities about all the murders. This woman, too, was tied with athletic tape. She was stashed under a tree in the woods. The body had still been warm when the officers arrived. A crimson carnation was thrust in her bound hands.

The FBI was involved and the autopsy would be done quickly. Emmanuel compared findings between the murders in Chesterfield and the one in Nottoway. There were just too many differences.

Shari was lighthearted when she left home. She loved the change in herself. Finally, after a long time, she was beginning to move forward, beginning to retrieve remnants of her old self. She wasn't deluded into believing that her relationship with Emmanuel would be a lasting one, although uncommitted sex went against her grain. Though she'd loved lovemaking before the incident, she'd never treated limited sexual intimacy casually.

Shari parked her car in the lot and made the long hike to her office. She was at her desk at nine and hunted down Walter. He was in the computer room patiently explaining something to a summer intern. A sickly hue still clung to his skin, and she wondered if he was coming down with something.

He straightened and glanced at her, doing a double take when he saw her. "Back already? Quick vacation."

"It didn't take long." She started to leave the computer room and Walter fell in step beside her.

"Exactly what took such a short time?"

"I rushed out of here in such a dither, I didn't tell anyone what I was doing. The police department believes Claudia Rhodes had a date with someone she met online the day she was murdered. I scanned her hard drive to retrieve e-mail messages.''

Walter's steps slowed. "Really?''

"Emmanuel's getting a warrant for the Internet provider to release the identity of her on-line lover.''

"I see.''

"I hope they find this man so that we can all get a good night's rest. I haven't been able to sleep well since her murder. This is such a small town, I thought it was safe.''

"Crime happens everywhere. But why do you think it's a computer date who killed her? It could have been anyone.''

"They don't know that he did it, but I guess he'll be one of the prime suspects. And there is that date.''

"Around the time she was killed?''

"Actually, if he was the one, he must have gotten to her earlier. Emmanuel doesn't talk too much about the case.''

"The computer date would be convenient for the police, I guess.''

Shari looked closely at him. She felt she had to defend Emmanuel. "Why do you say that? Emmanuel is trying to be thorough.''

"If they're focusing on the Internet date, it means the police won't lose time on finding out who may have really killed her.''

"Why do you think it wasn't him? Who else could it be? You sound protective of this man.''

"I'm not.'' He sighed, and waved a hand. "Just forget it. I don't know what I'm saying.''

"Anything happen while I was gone?"

"No. Everything ran smooth as rain."

"Good." She looked closely at him and frowned. "You really don't look very well at all. You haven't for the last few days. Have you seen a doctor yet?"

He shook his head. "No."

"Why don't you take time off? If you have something contagious, it could spread all over the office."

"I just might do that."

"Don't forget to make that doctor's appointment."

"Yeah, yeah."

"Men," she scoffed. "You hate taking care of yourselves."

Shari went to the cafeteria around one for a late lunch. The aromatic smell of the food made her mouth water. Since she usually lunched at her desk, she was surprised to see so many late diners. Kara and her boyfriend stood in line behind her.

The noise decreased several decibels when Jonathan strolled into the dining room. He made small talk with several of the employees, shook hands, and greeted workers. Then he grabbed a cup of coffee and perused the area. Shari knew the moment he spotted her because he headed to her table. Kara and Leon, the summer intern from Tuskegee, had just joined her at her table. Jonathan looked closely at the young man who glanced up uncertainly at him. "Don't you have work to do?" he asked, very unlike Jonathan.

"He's taking his lunch break." Shari didn't like

having her employees intimidated. What was up with him anyway?

Jonathan glanced at his watch. "Looks to me like lunch should be over," he said to the young man as if he hadn't seen the fifty or more people eating.

The young man's plate was full. Blake Industries offered free meals for summer interns.

Shari knew Leon had gotten a chemistry scholarship from the company and received a small salary from his summer job. Of course, Kara was Jonathan's niece and Jonathan was extremely protective, which was probably the purpose of his visit to the cafeteria.

"Jonathan . . ." Shari started.

"Uncle Jonathan . . ." Kara began in an annoyed tone. She was clearly embarrassed by her uncle's statement.

Leon stood. "Excuse me. I think I'll go back to my desk." He gathered his food and with his tray left the table.

Kari narrowed her eyes at her uncle. "I'm leaving, too."

"No need for you to leave, Kara," Jonathan said. "Sit down and finish your meal."

The younger woman pinched her lips and glared at her uncle. She packed her food and stood. "I wouldn't want to be accused of shirking on the job." She tilted her head and marched after Leon.

Jonathan frowned after them.

"Well," Shari said to break his scrutiny, "now that you've intimidated my lunch guests, how may I help you?"

He glanced at her as if he'd forgotten she was there. "May I join you?"

She waved her hand. "Help yourself."

Jonathan pulled out a chair and sank into it, setting his coffee on the table. "What are you doing here?"

"I'm all finished with the assignment. It didn't take long."

"I thought you were on vacation for a week."

A vacation hadn't been the gist of their conversation yesterday. "No. Only as long as it took me to complete the work."

Jonathan sipped his coffee and slowly placed the cup on the table. "I don't think you understood me. Either way, you're on vacation for two weeks."

"Two weeks? Jonathan, I don't need a vacation. I have work to do."

"I'm the boss, and I've looked at your records. You haven't had a day off in the year and a half that you've been here. We schedule vacations for a reason. People are less productive when they burn out."

Her stomach roiled. "I see. Do you have a problem with my performance?"

"No. And I want to keep it that way." He smiled and waved to an employee passing the table. "I'll see you in two weeks."

"Walter's off this afternoon. I can't leave."

"He'll be back tomorrow, won't he?"

"Yes, but . . ."

"And you can put someone else in charge for one afternoon, can't you?"

"Yes . . ."

"Good." Jonathan stood, shoved his chair under the table. "It's all settled."

"But . . ."

"Enjoy your time off." He dismissed her, turned and strolled across the room, dropping his Styrofoam cup into the trash. Shari stared openmouthed at his back.

What was that all about? she wondered as she finished her lonely lunch. She noticed several heads turned in her direction.

What was she going to do with two whole weeks off?

Chapter 9

Contrary to what Jonathan believed, leaving the office for two weeks took preparation. The head of a department couldn't just pick up her purse and disappear. For the next three hours, Shari made notes for Walter and completed projects that absolutely had to get out. Around four she took off her beeper and locked the door. It felt strange leaving work for two weeks when she'd purposely worked long hours the last couple of years.

She drove directly to the grocery store and bought makings for a salad. She'd taken chicken out of the freezer the night before to thaw. She'd prepare her special spiced chicken served with wild rice.

Clarice's and Gerald's reactions to her dating Emmanuel would be vastly different. She'd just sit back and let the fireworks fly. Shari knew that Gerald planned to grill her on Emmanuel. She could hold her own, but Gerald thought he should have a say in who she dated. She knew differently.

That was made very evident when he arrived first to dinner that evening. Shari's chicken was in the oven, sending delicious aromas through the house.

"Need any help?" Gerald asked, shucking his jacket and loosening his tie. Evidently he hadn't made it home to change before dinner.

"Sure. You could break up the lettuce for me."

After a quick trip to the bathroom to wash his hands, he came to the sink. Shari handed him a towel to tuck into his pants. She could just see him thinking about how to approach her on Emmanuel.

"Have you heard from Mom and Dad lately?" Shari asked before he got the chance to grill her.

He shrugged. "I called before I came here."

"I've been thinking about visiting them. How are they?" She handed him a tomato and started to grate a carrot.

"Good. April's having a baby."

Shari smiled. "You're kidding. I'm going to have to call her." April was the third sibling; she'd married two years ago. Shari had thought it would be another couple of years before she and her husband had children.

"They're pleased about another grandchild. Speaking of grandchildren," Gerald interjected smoothly, "Emmanuel will never marry you."

Shari scraped the carrots into a bowl and rinsed off the cutting board, knowing very well that her need to be a whole person again outweighed her need for lasting commitment. Gerald didn't know that. "Who says I'm looking for marriage?"

"You can't be satisfied with what he has to offer." Gerald's knife stilled on the tomato he was chopping.

"Lay off it, Gerald. Perhaps I need what he has to offer right now."

"He's offering nothing. A six-month relationship is worthless. He's not worth your time, Shari, because in a few months you'll be alone again anyway. And heartbroken. You don't take relationships lightly. Emmanuel does." He started slicing the tomato again. "He's a great police officer, but he's not a marrying man. I don't want the fallout you'll suffer once he drops you."

"Who says you'll get it? Please butt out," Shari said impatiently. "Being the youngest doesn't mean that I don't have enough sense to lead my own life. I know what kind of man Emmanuel is. We're just friends."

He gave her a narrow-eyed look. "Are you sure about that?"

She nodded, donning oven mitts to take the chicken out of the oven. "What else can there be?" Gerald had no idea she'd already experienced just about the worst, and it had nothing to do with Emmanuel.

He threw a weary glance her way. "Exactly."

The next morning, Shari's first inclination was to drive to Norfolk to visit her parents, but she'd visited them two weekends ago. They worked, and during the day she'd be around home alone. Still, she could have dinner cooked each evening when they arrived.

Two weeks. What was she going to do with two weeks? She could plan a vacation—Niagara Falls, Colorado, D.C.

Shari rubbed her hand across her forehead, realizing very well what she was doing. She was fleeing to give herself more time to think about Emmanuel—fleeing to elude him. Eventually, she'd talk herself out of the experience.

She didn't fear him. She was attracted to him. *Girlfriend, go with your feelings on this*, she said to herself in the mirror. She thought about her shapeless linen slacks and top. A victim's clothing. She was still acting like a victim. Change was so very difficult. She remembered Mrs. Golden who'd lived next door to her family when she was in high school. Each morning she'd rise at five-thirty, water the plants and read the paper before leaving for work at seven-thirty. Often she mentioned how much she hated rising so early. A few years later she retired and she continued to rise at five-thirty, water the plants and read the paper, even though she had no place to go. She had fallen into her routine. As long as she dealt with the familiar, life was manageable.

Perhaps familiarity was the reason Shari had held on to her clothing like a shield. Wearing unflattering outfits was her crutch, which she used to get through the years of healing. Perhaps it was time for her to throw away her crutch and get on with her life. And if she didn't change now, when would she? Next year, or the next?

She looked at her drab attire again. Rape was not about the clothing she wore or how she looked. She'd been told that enough times at the rape crisis center. But hearing the words was a world apart from believing them. She knew that it wasn't going to be as easy as changing her dress or slacks.

If she were to begin living her life again, the small-

est step would be her clothing. She had to start someplace and move on from there. She couldn't allow
herself time to think about it any longer. Snatching
her purse, she ran to her car and drove to Petersburg
to the mall a group of African-Americans reopened
several years after the major shopping center management moved out of the area. She went to the very
popular Paula's designer dress shop.

The store was bustling with shoppers. Paula greeted
her immediately. In Paula's, everyone was busy. You
never found a salesclerk gossiping about last night's
date or personal business when customers were
about. Paula believed the time for that was not in
her boutique.

The statuesque woman wore her natural hair cut
short and she wore a long flowing garment that hung
gracefully on her. "How did you like the green
dress?" Paula asked.

"It's beautiful," Shari responded, but didn't have
a clue where to begin shopping.

"So you *did* wear it on the cruise? Your sister was
worried."

"She needn't have been." Paula knew her customers and remembered their tastes.

Paula smiled. "What can I do for you today?"

"I'm replenishing my wardrobe."

"Just the kind of customer I love. You've come to
the right place." Paula glanced at her from head to
foot and ran her tongue over her teeth. "May I make
some suggestions?" she asked as she led the way to
the dress racks.

"Of course." Shari sighed and followed the
woman. This was the beginning of the new her, she
thought as Paula called someone to help her.

Paula selected outfits with practiced skill and an eye for elegance. She handed the items to her assistant. "Please put this in room two," she said, and proceeded to a rack of slacks, shorts, and blouses. Shari resigned herself to spending quite a long time in Paula's shop.

Walter popped a Tums into his mouth. He'd been down in the dumps since Claudia's death. Nothing he did seemed to relieve the ache that had planted itself deep into his heart.

How could he possibly visit the doctor's office where Claudia had worked when his past visits there had been such joy? Gazing upon Claudia's smiling face had lifted his heart. What could the doctor do anyway? As far as he knew, a cure for a broken heart had yet to be invented.

Instead, he drove to Gerald Jarrod's office for the appointment he'd made just before he left work. On the way, he drove past the park where Claudia's body had been discovered, and his stomach roiled.

He knew he should never have gotten involved with a married woman, and he hadn't. She was too much of a lady to indulge in an affair outside of her marriage. The distance separating them hadn't kept him from loving her. This budding desire had all started over the Internet—not the way most on-line dates began, but because of a very bad cold. He'd gone to the doctor whom she'd worked for, and through their conversation, she'd discovered he was a computer professional. She'd been having trouble with hers, besides the fact that she was a novice on the Internet and wanted to learn more. He'd shown her how to get started. Whenever she had a problem, she'd e-mail him.

It was just that simple. Before long, they were having long conversations over the Internet and he'd fallen in love with her. He made doctor's appointments just to feel her soft hand at his pulse. He'd gone to church to see her usher on fourth Sundays. But he'd never approached her or insinuated anything intimate because he respected her marriage. A week before she died, she'd told him that she'd asked her husband for a divorce. She was tired of his fooling around and wouldn't put her life on hold any longer. Then she said the words that were music to his heart. She'd told him she wanted to meet with him and asked about his feelings for her. He told her that he loved her and asked her to name the place. He'd be there.

Walter had really looked forward to their meeting. He'd gone to the flower shop and had bought a dozen roses—the ones she loved so much, not the cheap kind from a grocery store. When he'd arrived at the park, he carried the roses with him as a gift. A crowd stood in a wide circle and the police had barricaded the area. He'd glanced at his watch and watched for Claudia. He'd looked from a distance to seek out Claudia's face. He didn't see her.

He knew he couldn't get close because of the people crowded around. The longer he waited, the more worried he grew, until finally he approached the crowd and heard the whispers.

It was then that he'd realized there was a body in the police barricade and that it was Claudia. *She'd been murdered.* His world tumbled. In a daze he staggered back to his car and sat behind the wheel for what seemed like centuries before he'd gathered enough strength to leave. He didn't remember anything about his drive home, only his grief from his loss.

When he'd heard through the grapevine that the police had determined she'd had sexual intercourse before she died, he remembered that she'd told him that the intimacy with her husband had ceased long ago. So whoever killed her had not just had sex with her. He'd raped her.

He'd wanted only the best for her, and she'd gotten the worse from someone. All her tender regard and warm smiles for the many patients who came to the office were no more.

He pressed his hand over his chest. The weight that had lodged there since Claudia's death felt as if it planned to remain for the duration.

So many worries plagued him. There was his mother. If he got himself arrested, it would just kill her. His brother had caused her untold worry, staying in trouble, refusing to do right, even in high school. Everything she ever said to his brother seemed to go in one ear and out the other. Sometimes he'd heard her crying late into the night. He'd go in and comfort her, promising things would get better, but they never got better, and now his brother was dead. He'd vowed to himself never to cause her worry. Never to cause anything other than happy tears to stream from her eyes. And now he was destined for the same kind of trouble that befell his brother. He closed his eyes briefly. He couldn't disappoint her that way.

Walter parked the car in downtown Nottoway. Sighing deeply with the worry that dragged his spirits, he walked slowly into the office of the lawyer he'd chosen.

"Pleasure to meet you, Mr. Lamar." Gerald Jarrod strolled around the desk and shook hands with Walter. Then he motioned him to a chair.

"Thank you for seeing me on short notice." Walter slid into the seat. "I work with your sister Shari at Blake Industries."

"I remember meeting you at the Christmas party," Gerald said, dropping into his own seat behind the desk. "How may I help you?" He leaned back into his leather chair.

"I'm sure you read about Claudia Rhodes's murder."

"Yes, I did."

"Well, I was supposed to meet her at the park around eleven-thirty. It was across the street from her job. Convenient."

Gerald nodded. "I see."

"But I didn't kill her. I wasn't there when she was murdered, or I'd have protected her. It was our first official meeting. I'd been in love with her for a while, but she was married and I wouldn't approach her. We did converse often over the Internet."

"Why do you think they'll want you?"

"I know that your sister scanned the disk on Claudia's computer to discover her chat partner. They'll find it was me almost immediately." Walter told him about his association with Claudia, and Gerald stopped him many times with pointed questions.

"I'll represent you, and I'll give Emmanuel a call," Gerald said. "You go home. If they do approach you, call me and I'll be there in ten minutes. Don't say anything until I get there."

Gerald stood, and so did Walter, accepting the business card Gerald held out. They shook hands, and Gerald walked him to the door.

"Don't worry now."

Walter did worry as he went to the car, but the weight that had settled on his chest lessened somewhat. He didn't have to deal with all of it on his own any longer. And he felt somehow better. Not much—but some.

Emmanuel had contacted the local FBI office in Richmond to get the screen name from the Internet provider. He was getting ready to leave the office when his mother called.

"Emmanuel, baby, you do remember the family day at Kings Dominion, don't you?"

Oh, shit, Emmanuel thought. "When?"

"Day after tomorrow." He heard disapproval over the phone line. "You did forget, didn't you? You missed out last year. I want you to go with the rest of the family this year. Everyone was there except you."

"All right, I'll be there."

"Jonathan's renting a minibus tomorrow. Seats twenty."

"I'll drive."

"Nope. That was your excuse last year. And you ended up not coming at all. It's a family day for a reason. And it won't be too busy because it's a weekday. I expect you to be on the bus, baby."

Emmanuel thought about the cramped bus loaded with fifteen or sixteen people—everyone sandwiched up together. Johanna and Mamma fighting, the kids screaming. He could take family, but in very small doses. Not all at once.

"I promise you I'll be there," he said reluctantly, "if you stop calling me baby."

"I don't know why you get so bent out of shape. You'll always be my baby. Besides, the ride is more than traveling there. It's an opportunity to spend time with the family."

Emmanuel groaned. He knew that.

"Why don't you invite Clarice's sister? Shari, I think her name is."

Emmanuel knew a snow job when he heard it. His mom was good at using strategies to get what she wanted.

"Or if you're too busy, I can invite her along. There's enough room, baby. Karl and Karlton are driving one of their cars."

"Thank goodness for small favors," Emmanuel whispered.

"What was that?"

"Nothing." That only left about a thousand other kids and grown-ups in the car. "By the time you add the boyfriends, there won't be room."

"I saved two seats especially for you. I've got the list right here."

"All right, all right. I'll be there. Tell Jonathan I'll drive." At least up front he didn't have to deal with whatever was going on in the back. He'd just take earphones along.

After he disconnected, he tried to reach Shari but she didn't answer. He left a message for her to call him. He hoped she hadn't skipped town.

* * *

By the time Emmanuel left the office, it was ten and Shari hadn't returned his call. He knew that Shari was probably in bed, but he drove by her house anyway. The light was on and his heart skipped a beat. Knowing that single women might be alarmed by getting a knock this late, he picked up his cell phone and called her. She answered on the second ring.

"Thought you'd be in bed early for work tomorrow," he said. She seemed happy to hear from him.

"I'm on a forced vacation."

"What are you doing on vacation? Are you going anyplace?" Jonathan had come through for him.

"I don't know," she answered. "Right now, I'm debating."

"I certainly would love to see you."

"Well, come by. What time are you leaving the office?"

"I've already left, I'm pulling into your driveway right now."

"You're kidding."

"Nope. Be there in a sec," he said, and disconnected.

She opened the door and he stepped into the kitchen. To the left he saw bags and bags and bags of clothing.

"What did you do? Buy out the store?"

"Seems like it, doesn't it? Well, I shopped, then stopped by the Women's Center. I just got here a few minutes ago."

"Thought you were on vacation."

"I am," she said, loading up with bags.

He started grabbing bags. "Why don't I help you?" When she opened her mouth, he said, continuing to load up, "Otherwise you'll spend your entire night upstairs."

They trooped up the stairs to her bedroom and added the bags to what she'd already carried up.

"Jeez," Emmanuel exclaimed, wondering if Johanna had invested money for him. This was going to be one expensive woman, he thought. He also had the feeling she'd be worth it. "So what's in all these bags?" He swiped a hand toward the bags and took in the feminine room, including the teddy bear on her bed. She could always cuddle up with him.

"Some more things. I have to hang these up, or they'll be wrinkled."

"Need help?"

She shook her head. "You can get soda, or something from the fridge. I'll only be a moment."

"I'd rather watch you," he said, and sat on the padded rocker. The patchwork fabric matched the spread. Feminine blue curtains hung at the open window.

She looked as if she were going to force him out, then she checked herself and said, "Okay," and proceeded to unpack bag after bag of colorful garments.

He smiled and enjoyed the view. Did he have anything to do with the change? If so, great! He crossed his ankle over his knee and watched her. He couldn't wait to see her in those numbers. If he had any say in it, she wouldn't be going on vacation anytime soon.

"So how did your day go?" she asked.

"Busy. I don't want to talk shop, though."

She stopped the motion of hanging a red dress

that would look magnificent against her brown skin. "What do you want to talk about?"

He shrugged. He was satisfied with just watching her and unwinding. He wished he could take some time off to spend with her, but Claudia's case couldn't wait. "The family's taking a trip to Kings Dominion. Will you go with me?" he asked.

"I love riding the coasters. You're not chicken, are you?"

A woman after his own heart. "Me? I'll keep you on them all day."

The day of the family trip dawned hot and muggy. Emmanuel was pleased that Shari hadn't left town. She agreed to go with him, and he only hoped being with his family wouldn't frighten her away. But then she had sisters and brothers, so she knew the way of large families.

He was also pleased that he was driving. Shari sat in the passenger seat across from him. His mom and dad took seats midway back. Mom had her arms crossed in a satisfied pose. She'd gotten what she wanted.

Pam's two daughters and their boyfriends sat near the back. Kara and Leon sat near them. Jonathan and Johanna sat across from Emmanuel's mom and dad. Jonathan wisely chose the aisle seat to separate the women. That left the kids right in back of Emmanuel. *Just great,* he thought. Already two kids were kicking his seat. Emmanuel wanted to tear out his own hair before he remembered he was almost bald. Today was going to be one very long day, he thought as he glanced over at Shari. She had turned around to answer a question Jonathan had asked her. Emmanuel would have to thank Jonathan for forcing this vacation on Shari. Now she was all his for two weeks.

"Everybody got everything?" Emmanuel asked before he closed the door. The girls had already made trips back to the car for something. They never got off anywhere on time.

Karl's yellow Mustang pulled up beside the bus and Karl tooted the horn. Karlton leaned down in the seat, his shoulder abutting Monica's, his arm resting on her thigh. He spotted Emmanuel and waved his other hand. Emmanuel shook his fist at him. Karlton grinned.

"When are we going to go?" Johanna asked. "I'm ready."

"We all are."

Emmanuel started the bus and put it in gear. The Mustang tore out in front of them. In the bus, Emmanuel stirred to a sluggish start.

The trip to the park had been everything that Emmanuel had envisioned, but once they arrived, the situation improved. His mom said she and his dad were spending the day in the kiddy park with the kids. Last year Jonathan had taken care of them. This year she ordered Jonathan to have fun. The girls went off on their own with their dates, but not before Johanna handed them a schedule. Each couple was to spend an hour with the children to relieve the grandparents.

But there were always snafus. The first one started at the gate when the guard wanted to check Gladys's bag. She told him her bag was none of his business, and she wasn't going to spend good money to be treated like a criminal. Jonathan quickly intervened to stymie a riot because Gladys wasn't above starting one if it was needed. At last they'd made it in.

Emmanuel took his schedule from Johanna and said good-bye, tugging Shari along with him. Jonathan, Johanna, James, and Pamela escorted Gladys and Henry Jones to the kiddy park.

As everyone disappeared, the tension drained out of Emmanuel.

"You've got a nice family, Emmanuel," Shari remarked.

"They're okay." And they were really. He was the one with the problem. Emmanuel rubbed his hands together. "All right. Are you ready for coasters?"

Shari raised a challenging brow. "I'm ready. Are you?"

"I bet you're chicken," he said.

Shari scowled at him. "Not me," she said, and checked the map for directions. When they arrived, a line had already formed. They meandered slowly along the rail.

For the first time, Emmanuel cleared his mind and took in the outfit Shari wore. How on earth could he have missed the green shorts and sleeveless print top? Especially with her great legs revealed. She wore short white socks and shiny white tennis shoes. She'd left her shoulder-length black hair unbound, but covered with a straw hat.

He smiled at her.

She cocked her head to the side. "What?"

"You've got"—he neared her and put his hands

on either side of the railing behind her"—beautiful legs."

She smiled a coy smile. "Think so?" She linked her hands at his waist.

"Yeah, I know so," he whispered, enjoying the feel of her hands on him. He caressed a finger along her face. This was not the place to make out, but desire for this woman was clouding his senses.

"Hey, Uncle E."

Emmanuel spun around. Karlton and Karl came walking up the plank with their girlfriends. His niece had a knowing smile on her face. Karlton's arm was around her shoulder as they leaned into each other when they came to a halt. With his girlfriend glued to his waist Karl chomped on his gum. She wasn't the same girl Karl had backed against the pinball machine in the sports bar.

"You all couldn't find another ride?" Emmanuel asked, annoyed at their intrusion. He was trying to avoid his family.

Karlton shrugged his shoulders. "This one's the best." Then he leaned against the railing next to Shari, pulling his girl against his side. Emmanuel stifled the impulse to snatch his niece away and hide her until she was thirty and the boy had developed some sense, but Shari struck up a conversation with the kids. They seemed to like her.

It took ten minutes to make it through the hair-raising ride. Emmanuel wanted another whirl, but Shari didn't. The boys went back in line and Emmanuel pulled Shari to another ride. They rode ride after ride until their throats grew dry. Then they stopped at a lemonade stand for drinks and started riding again until it was their turn to stay with the kids.

Gladys and Henry were cooling themselves under a shade tree sipping on bottled water.

"Where're the kids?" Emmanuel said.

"The boys came to get them. They got tired of these rides. They said they'd bring them right back." Gladys glanced at her watch. "I certainly didn't want to let them out of my sight, but Henry said they should be okay."

Just then Emmanuel heard a whoop and some screaming cheers. He looked across the way to the hyped-up kids with the boys and their dates. They were probably loaded with sugar. And they were dripping wet.

"Y'all have fun?" Henry asked the little ones.

"We had a good time, Grandpa." Their eyes were glassy, and they couldn't stand still.

"Oh, you're a bunch of dirty waifs," Gladys said, pulling out her baby wipes and swiping down mouths and hands.

By seven, everyone was so exhausted, they were dragging. Jonathan ended up carrying Terri back to the van. Emmanuel and Shari slowly made their way back to the gate. They had stopped to get a strawberry waffle cream when Emmanuel spotted Howard and the woman he'd seen at his house the night he went to interview him. The two walked around arm in arm, as if they were having a mighty grand time.

Emmanuel came to a halt.

Shari almost dropped her plate. She glanced up at him. "What's wrong?" she asked.

Emmanuel frowned after the couple. Then he

tugged Shari into step again. "I saw Howard with someone."

"Who?"

"I don't know." But he did have her name in his notebook. He'd do a check on her because she worked for the company that had provided an alibi for Howard the day Claudia was killed. Women had clung to Howard at the funeral offering support and anything else, but from the beginning those women were already out of the running. It seemed Howard had his next wife already picked out.

Shari placed a spoonful of ice cream and strawberries with the waffle in his mouth. He chewed on the delicious concoction and thought about Claudia.

Chapter 10

At the station, Emmanuel played back his messages. It shouldn't have surprised him to find one from Gerald Jarrod. Probably called to warn Emmanuel off his sister. Emmanuel would have been a lot more receptive to getting a call from his sister. Shari was too old for her brother to be issuing sibling warnings. Nonetheless, he glanced at the watch and saw that it was six-thirty. He was about to pick up the phone to answer his messages when an officer came in with an envelope.

"You were waiting for this," he said.

Emmanuel took the package from him. Copies of several e-mail messages were inside, correspondence between Claudia and her chat friend. The name of the user was Walter Lamar, and he lived in Nottoway. Claudia had written to him that her relationship with Howard was over, that she'd asked him for a divorce.

They made a date to meet in the park at eleven-thirty the day Claudia was murdered. The fact that he was scheduled to meet her, in and of itself wasn't damning. After all, she'd made an appointment with Emmanuel, as well. What puzzled Emmanuel was why Lamar hadn't come forward. Many people didn't trust the police department, but the Nottoway department strived for fairness and truth for everyone.

Claudia's e-mail messages actually were more detrimental to Howard. Emanuel would have to interview Howard again.

Emmanuel grabbed his jacket and started for the door. He was on his way when he remembered that he hadn't called Gerald. He retraced his steps, to the phone and dialed the number, glancing at his watch again. Emmanuel thought Gerald had probably left for home by now, but to Emmanuel's surpise, he answered.

"I've been trying to reach you," Gerald said.

Emmanuel waited for the lecture, but he was shocked when Gerald mentioned Walter's name and identified him as his client.

"Mr. Lamar was due to meet her that morning. He didn't come forward for fear of being blamed for her death. He's deeply upset and would like to help the department in any way that he can. He can't offer very much outside of their mail messages. They'd never met on a personal level. He's willing to meet with you," Gerald continued.

"We'd like to talk with him. Could you bring him to the station tomorrow morning?"

"We'll be there at eight," Gerald assured him, and hung up.

* * *

On his way to purchase tickets for the movie he was taking Shari to see, Emmanuel stopped by Howard's house. He waited for a half hour but Howard didn't show up. No telling when he'd be home. The man hadn't called once to find out about the investigation of Claudia's murder.

Emmanuel left. He'd call back tomorrow and spend half of the day in the office.

After the long wait for the tickets, he tucked them into his pocket and drove home with just enough time to shower and dress before heading to Shari's.

Emmanuel was casually dressed in jeans, a dark blue shirt, and sports jacket. The jacket was in deference to dinner after the movie.

Shari met him at the door wearing tailored royal blue linen slacks and a matching sleeveless shirt with a V neck.

Emmanuel was surprised to see so much exposed skin and so many curves, and he looked her up and down. "You look good enough to eat," he said.

Shari smiled. "You're looking quite handsome yourself."

"May I kiss you?" he asked, already tugging her to him.

She nodded and smiled. "Yes, you may," she said with a slow seductive note in her voice.

Desire already curled in him. In a smooth movement he gathered her in his arms and kissed her solidly. Her desire spilled over like a rapidly flooding river.

"Why don't we forget the movie?" Emmanuel mumbled against her mouth.

"You've talked about that movie forever."

He nuzzled her neck, loving the subtle scent she wore, the softness of her skin. "There are other things I'd enjoy more than movies."

"And I bet I could never guess what they are."

Emmanuel chuckled and loosened his grip. Shari moved away from him and grabbed her jacket from the back of a chair.

When they reached the theater, the line was so long, it reached out into the street. Everybody and their mother arrived for the first showing of *Remember The Titans* starring Denzel Washington. Even Mrs. Drucilla and Luke were there. Age gave them status in Nottoway. They weren't allowed to stand outside. The seniors were immediately motioned inside for the seats of their choice.

After the movie, Emmanuel and Shari went directly to Karina's restaurant. Karina's daughter and her friend Monica, Emmanuel's niece, were hostesses because the regular hostess called in sick. Monica showed them to their table and handed them menus. They were seated in a quiet area where the light was muted, casting an intimate glow.

"Ah . . . Uncle Emmanuel, can we all stay at your place tomorrow night?"

He hadn't recovered from the family trip to King's Dominion yet. "I'm working tomorrow."

"You're not working tomorrow night, are you? It's the weekend."

"Since when did crime stop for weekends?" He glanced at Shari and hoped he wouldn't be working that night. "I may not be working that night, but I'm not baby-sitting, either."

"But you promised." They came up with more fibs.

"No, I didn't." Emmanuel snapped his menu open.

His niece was persistent. "You said we could stay over a couple of times this summer. The summer's half-over. I'll be leaving for college soon."

Emmanuel sighed and thought about his empty cupboards. Then he looked into his niece's sorrowful, hopeful eyes and wondered what the hell she was up to. He knew he was going to regret this, but he was a sucker for his nieces and nephews, even though en masse they drove him crazy. "Okay."

The smile on her face alarmed him. "Thanks, Uncle E," she said, hugging him. "Kara's coming, too, okay?"

Emmanuel threw a disgusted glance her way that had no effect on her. "With the whole platoon, what's one more?"

She rushed away.

"Tell her brothers I better not see either of them within two miles of my property." Although Karlton, the more serious triplet, was dating Monica, the boy knew how to push Emmanuel's buttons and used every opportunity to do so.

"Oh, Uncle E." She rolled her eyes, trying to look dignified as she sailed toward the foyer, but failed miserably.

Emmanuel frowned after her. "I wonder what that's all about." But mostly he was thinking that he wouldn't be able to snuggle up with Shari tomorrow night like he'd planned. With this case, they'd had so little time together as it was. He'd been hoping to make some progress while she was on vacation.

Shari glanced up from her menu. "Whatever it is, you won't like it," she said with a knowing smile.

Emmanuel reached across the table, lifted Shari's hand, and kissed the knuckle. "I'm not going to worry about it tonight. There's always tomorrow."

Emmanuel opened the door for Shari and escorted her into the house. Her scent had driven him crazy all night. As much as he wanted to reintroduce her slowly to the pleasures a man and woman had to offer each other, the more time they spent together, the more difficult it was to leave her at the door with only a chaste kiss. But leave her he would until she was ready. When their time came, it would be Fourth of July fireworks.

He tugged her into his arms knowing that within a couple of minutes he'd leave her at the door and return to his own lonely house to spend the night. When he linked his arms around her and pulled her closer to him, she surprised him by responding completely to him. He pressed her against him, holding her body tightly against his.

He tried to keep himself under control, to remember her fragility, but it had been a while for him and the spiraling warmth curling in his stomach was sweet.

He felt her hand moving along his back, stroking his skin, and he forgot to listen to his brain. He was consumed with a need that flowed wild and hot through his body. It seemed he'd waited forever to hold this sweetness in his arms.

He ran his hands over her soft skin, and he let himself luxuriate in the pleasure of her touches.

Emmanuel deepened the kiss, sucking delicately on her tongue.

"We fit perfectly together," he whispered against her lips. "Take my shirt off." He kissed her forehead, giving her a chance to stop, yet needing to know if she was as ready for him as he was for her.

Her hands tentatively slid up his chest. When he felt the first button release, he inhaled sharply.

"Are you okay with this?"

"Yes," she whispered as she continued to undo the buttons and slid the shirt off his shoulders. Her warm touch sent sensations of burning desire flashing through him.

He kissed her again, tugging her shirt up to cup her breasts. Suddenly she tugged his shirt and jacket off his shoulders. Unnoticed, they dropped to the floor.

Like a dance to a ballad, he pulled her shirt over her head, unhooked her bra, and pressed her breasts against his chest. He loved the texture, the softness, the difference that made her so special. He leaned lower to capture her breast in his mouth, sucking gently on a nipple. Better than dinner, he thought as he wrapped his hands around her waist and stroked her hips.

Shari ran her fingers over the muscles rippling on his shoulder. He lifted her in his arms and carried her up the stairs, into the bedroom, and deposited her onto the bed. He flipped on the bedside light. The gentle illumination from the lamp highlighted her glowing body. He leaned down, unsnapped her pants and pulled them down her hips, down her long legs to drop on the floor.

He lay down beside her and brought her on top of him, letting her set the pace of their loving.

Shari hesitated at first but he guided her mouth to his. She liked the taste of him—the light cologne he wore, the texture of his skin against her breasts. The contrasting texture of hair, skin, muscle.

He smoothed his hands down her lithe back. The staccato beat of his heart accelerated as he watched her with half-closed lids, easily taking her weight, letting her explore his body and touching hers, driving her insane with desire.

Shari decided she liked leading as she bent and glided her tongue slowly over his chin. His deep, masculine groan gave her courage. He touched every inch of her body. His movements were controlled, delicious, unhurried. His hands caressed her hips, ran along the back of her thighs, driving her wild, but not entering her.

She wanted his fingers in her; she wanted him. Large masculine hands explored and tempted—sent delightful sensations along her spine. His tongue traced the fullness of her lips and found its way back inside, dueling with hers. Then they parted.

They gazed at each other. Breaths quickened. She slid down his body and unbuckled his pants and slid them down his hips along with his jockeys.

"Touch me," he entreated.

She stroked the masculine strength of him. He was pure male perfection.

She never knew a kiss could be so sensual, a touch so exotic. The tempo was quick then slow. Her desire grew to a fever pitch. He tugged her panties down her legs, searched in his pockets for a foil package. Shari took it from him and stroked him as she slid on the prophylactic. She'd never done this before, and found the gesture intensely erotic.

Then he lifted her onto his hips and positioned himself at her opening. She was tight, but they slowly merged, his hands splaying her hips than her thighs. His thrusts were slow at first and then powerful. Fever built. His hands moved to her hips and he ground his hips up to thrust deeply while she met him with equal fervor. As they moved, he stroked her body.

They moved in cadence until the world spiraled and she crashed to his chest. He held her close to him as she slowly slid back to earth.

She never realized that loving could be so sweet.

Except for the glow of the full moon in her bedroom window, it was still dark outside. Emmanuel's arm was thrown around Shari's waist. He'd slept peacefully and she had, too, until the weight of his arm around her startled her awake. She was accustomed to sleeping alone. She turned to face him. When she'd realized it was Emmanuel, her heartbeat had returned to normal. His breathing was slow and deep. The covers had fallen and revealed the dark hair on his chest. She pulled the covers up to cover her breasts and tried to assess her feelings for what had happened.

All this time, she'd tried to convince herself that the attraction was there, that their lovemaking would be an experiment. But Shari realized that she hadn't made love with this man simply to see if she could. That notion was against all her ingrained principles.

She'd made love with him for one reason only: She was stupidly falling in love with him.

Stupidly because Emmanuel would never love her in turn. Six months—if she were lucky, a year. Then he'd be moving on to his next conquest. But then, he had never promised her tomorrow. He had never promised forever. And from the beginning she knew to expect only what he was willing to give.

Shari sighed. She wished she could be one of those women who could take pleasure in lovemaking just for pleasure sake. She was cursed with needing more—needing it to lead somewhere.

At six, Shari cooked a big breakfast for Emmanuel while he showered. They'd made love again before they'd climbed out of bed. Anxiety crawled up her back.

As she cut up pieces of ham for the omelet, she heard the shower turn off and his baritone voice singing a love song. Shari smiled. He'd never be Lou Rawls but his singing was pleasant to her ears. She'd slept better last night than she had in a very long time.

Then her smile faltered. When she'd visited his home, he'd said that a woman had never stayed the night there. She cut up the last of the ham and set it aside. Was she simply one in many women to him? After they'd part, would he say the same thing to the next woman? "Stop it, Shari," she said to the empty room.

"What was that?" Emmanuel called.

She yelled up, "Nothing."

"I'll be right out," he shouted from the bathroom. Then he went back to his disjointed singing.

Shari grabbed the frying pan and turned on the heat. Then she beat the eggs and poured them into the pan. She wasn't going to think herself out of this relationship. She enjoyed his company. He was a patient lover. Just the kind she needed to get over her hurt. For once in her life, she was going to enjoy the here and now, she thought as she flipped the omelet and piled on cheese and ham.

She heard him descending the stairs. As he came into the room, he grabbed her around her waist and kissed her on the neck.

"Good morning," he whispered.

"A good morning to you, Mr. Jones," Shari said as she dished the omelet onto the plate.

"That looks good and smells wonderful."

She handed the plate to him. "Enjoy it while it's nice and hot."

"Where's yours?" he asked as he took the plate from her.

"I'll make another one."

"Share this one with me. With the pancakes, this will be enough."

She faced him. "Are you sure?"

He cut the omelet and put half on another plate. She set the pancakes and maple syrup on the table. The cranberry juice and coffee were already there.

They sat at the round table. Emmanuel pulled his chair close to hers. He said grace. Shari topped the pancakes with maple syrup and whipped cream.

"Will you come over tonight?" he asked. "You won't have to work. I just want to see you."

"Sure. What shall I bring?" she asked as she sliced a bite of pancake.

"Just you . . . in a bathing suit."

Shari chuckled. "I'll bring the bathing suit with me."

"You want to model it for me before I leave?"

"I'll surprise you."

"Damn, I can't wait for tonight."

Shari drew a finger along his jaw. "I bought a new two-piece at Paula's."

Emmanuel gulped his juice and frowned at her. "You know how to torture a man, don't you?"

"It's called anticipation." She sipped her coffee.

"It's called torture," Emmanuel corrected.

Shari smiled coyly.

"Bet you love torturing men."

"I don't call it torture," she murmured, setting her cup down. "Why do you have to go in anyway?"

"I forgot to tell you I got Claudia's chat partner's name just before I left the station. He lives here."

"Who is it?"

"He must be a newcomer because I don't know him. He's Walter Lamar."

Shari dropped her fork on her plate.

"What's wrong? Do you know him?"

"He works with me."

"I knew he worked at Blake Industries, but . . ."

"I can't believe it! He's the assistant manager of my department. Have you arrested him?"

"I don't have anything to arrest him on yet. But he's hired Gerald. Your brother's bringing him in for questioning this morning"—he glanced at the clock—"at eight."

The breakfast Shari was enjoying was forgotten as

she leaned her head on her steepled fingers. "I can't believe this is happening again."

"Nothing's happened yet. There's nothing to prove that he did anything. We're questioning anyone who may have had some contact with her or who may be able to provide useful information. Don't jump to conclusions, okay?"

"I'm not. It's just you think you know a person. Simon was nothing like Walter. Walter is always so kind—so thoughtful. I can just say aloud that I wish I had a program for something, and a week later he delivers it to me. He's a fabulous worker. It's just . . ."

"What about Simon?"

"He was so competitive. Competition is a good thing, but he carried it to the extreme. He was argumentative and hated it when women got raises or higher positions than him. He thought he deserved to run the place. I was his project leader and it was always a fight with him. But after a while he calmed down and we were able to work together with some degree of cooperation." Shari grabbed a napkin and wiped her mouth. "Was I wrong?"

Emmanuel gathered her hand in his and stroked the back. "Every man you encounter isn't a rapist."

"Intellectually I know that. I grew up with a loving father and wonderful brothers, even though we fought a lot. But they always respected women, so I don't have misconceptions on that score."

Emmanuel slid his chair close to hers and put an arm around her. "I'm doing the best that I can to find Claudia's murderer. I want you safe." He still thought of Howard and the woman he spent the day with at Kings Dominion. Howard didn't even allow himself a grieving period. It was relatively safe to say that he probably didn't need it.

Shari rubbed her temple. Finding out the suspect was Walter hit so close to home, just like before. "Maybe it's some copycat," she said, hoping her judgment wasn't so far-fetched. Could she trust her own assessment any longer?

Emmanuel nodded his head. "It's not a serial killer's work—just made to appear like one. It's a copycat."

With trepidation, Emmanuel left Shari to change clothes at his home before driving to the office. He made it there with ten minutes to spare.

Both Gerald and Walter wore power suits to the office. Both were tall, commanding, professional African-American men.

Gerald shook Emmanuel's hand, and so did Walter before they took seats in his office.

"May I get you coffee? It's not the best, but it'll wake you up."

They nodded. Emmanuel went to the pot, poured coffee into Styrofoam cups, and brought them back to the men along with a couple of packages of sugar and powdered cream.

Gardell entered the room carrying his own coffee, shut the door, and then took a seat.

Emmanuel began the questioning—many questions which had been asked of other interviewees, and a few pointed ones only Walter could answer. He didn't learn anything new. He merely asked Walter not to leave town in case they had more questions for him.

Chapter 11

Around noon Emmanuel ran to the supermarket and bought enough food to last the kids through lunch the next day, at which time they should head home. Girls liked snacks they could munch on through the night. His nephews weren't teenagers yet, so he didn't have to buy out the store to feed them. Still, he threw in a few extra bags of chips and pretzels, a huge box of hamburgers, and packages of hot dogs. After he put it all away, he posted a DO NOT ENTER sign on his bedroom door, and returned to work. The kids would start rolling in around five. He should be home in plenty of time.

Long ago Emmanuel learned that schedules rarely ran according to plan. Just before he arrived at the office, someone called in a report that a huge accident had occurred on Loco Road where teenagers had been racing. Emmanuel responded and turned

the SUV in that direction. It took less than five minutes of hard driving. On his way there, he feared what
he'd find. Although the triplets got on his last nerve,
underneath he liked the boys, and tension gripped
his chest at the thought that something may have
happened to them.

Phoenix was in town and they usually laid low when
their father was around. Still, Loco Road was isolated
and they could have tried their luck. When Emmanuel arrived, someone had helped the teens out of
the cars. Thank goodness Karl and Karlton weren't
involved, and there was nothing more serious than
a few bumps on their tough heads, scratches, and
sprained wrists. He was in for a very long afternoon.
The ambulance transported them all to the hospital,
but it took hours to get the cars out of the deep
ravine and deal with the other uninjured teenagers
and their parents. About seven cars had been at the
scene.

By four-thirty Emmanuel was still in the office filling out reports, so he called Shari. Behind him, the
noise of parents screaming at their kids was so loud
that he had to cover his other ear to hear.

"I hate to lay this on you, but I'm running later
than I thought."

"That's okay. Clarice said her kids were coming
over, so I'll just pick them up on my way."

"They are?" This was news to Emmanuel.

"You didn't know?"

How many more surprises lay ahead? "The more
the merrier," he told Shari, glad that he'd brought
extra food. He made a mental note to take some
Tylenol to get him through the night, and told Shari
the hiding place for his key.

As soon as Shari hung up, she called her sister, telling her she'd pick up the kids. She quickly changed into shorts, grabbed her bathing suit, and made the short drive to Clarice's. The kids were so happy, they were overflowing with energy. They ran to the front door with duffel bags and sleeping bags. They must not have heard Emmanuel's warning about the candy. At this point, Shari certainly wasn't going to warn them.

"We're ready," Chantel said.

"Let's go, Auntie," Tylan, Jr., said, pulling on Shari's hand.

"Wait a minute," Clarice said. "Don't I get a kiss and hug?"

Tylan, Jr., rolled his eyes, but went to his mom for the hug. At eight, he wouldn't admit he still liked hugs from his mom.

"The car door's open," Shari said to him, and he streaked out of the house with his burden.

Chantel eagerly ran into her mother's arms. "I'm only going for one night. You're gonna call me?" she asked hopefully.

"Tonight at eight," Clarice assured her. Satisfied, the child ran after her brother.

"Wait for me," she yelled, struggling with her load.

Clarice smiled as she watched her children. "Tylan will drive over with the go-carts later."

"What for?" Shari could imagine the look on Emmanuel's face when he saw go-carts.

"Phyllis called. She told them all the kids are taking them."

Shari was well aware of Emmanuel's reticence with children. The kids would have fun, but they were going to drive him up the wall. His quiet little world would turn into a madhouse. Shari shrugged. Emmanuel was big enough to take it.

"Mrs. Drucilla baked corn pudding for the children to take with them. You make sure you get a dish," Clarice said on her way to the kitchen. Clarice dug the foil-covered dish out of the fridge and handed it to Shari.

"Everyone loves Mrs. Drucilla's corn pudding. I'll probably go over tomorrow morning and help Emmanuel with breakfast," Shari said. "I'll bring them home."

"No need. Mrs. Drucilla and Luke will pick them up on their way to Richmond. They're spending a couple of days with Tylan's folks."

"You and Tylan be sure to enjoy your vacation."

"As soon as you leave, I'm starting my vacation in a hot bubble bath."

Shari laughed. "In that case, I won't keep you."

When Shari arrived at Emmanuel's place, all three of the triplets' cars were parked outside. Karlton was chasing after Monica. She screeched, dodging him. He let her get a little distance before his long legs caught up. He lifted her in the air and kissed her.

Shari groaned. Keeping the boys at a distance was Emmanuel's greatest wish, but he wasn't going to get it.

Her niece and nephew spotted Phyllis and Monica's two brothers and clamored out of the car, forgetting their bedrolls and bags.

Shari got out after them and went around the back of the house and got the key from the flower pot. She hustled back to the front door, and opened it.

Everyone knew their place. The girls went upstairs

and commandeered their area. The boys dumped their sleeping bags and duffel bags in a corner in the great room. Then Kara got the teenagers to move the sofa and furniture to the side to make room for the boys to sleep.

Shari looked at Karl. "You aren't spending the night, are you?"

"Just part of it," he said, dodging to the glass door out back accompanied by a teen with her skirt too tight and too short, her bustier showing too much.

Shari had to admit the girl was beautiful. Just the kind Emmanuel probably had gone after at that age. She looked down at her serviceable jean shorts and demure top. She wouldn't pass for anybody's hot number.

In the corner Karlton straightened up the couches and arranged a conversational area so that the room at least looked decent.

Kara and Monica came bouncing down the stairs wearing bikinis. "I don't know about you all, but I'm heading to the Jacuzzi," Monica announced.

"I'm with you," Karlton said, sliding his jean shorts down. For a moment, Shari just about had a heart attack, until she realized that he wore swim trunks underneath.

The kids dashed to the bathroom, and scampered into their swimwear. Within minutes everyone disappeared outside.

Somebody yelled that they were hungry. Shari looked in the refrigerator, saw that Emmanuel had loaded up on hamburgers and hot dogs, so she took the meat out, put it on the countertop, and went out back to start up the gas grill.

* * *

Emmanuel made one last trip to Howard's house before he started home. The man was still out of town. The insurance money hadn't been released yet, so he'd be back.

Emmanuel continued to wait for the test results and the meaning of the microscopic details the forensic examiner discovered at the autopsy. He had certainly hoped to resolve things sooner than this.

As he neared his turnoff and drove the long lane to his house, bright lights shown outside. Before he cleared the trees, he heard a boom box blaring from somewhere. Suddenly he stood on his brakes. Six go-carts streaked across his lawn, then turned the corner to round his house in a heated race. Emmanuel eased his SUV to the left and parked between two trees, a safe distance from the kids. When he exited, he tightened his lips. Two familiar Mustangs that shouldn't be anywhere near his home were parked under his carport.

He slammed the door, skirted the house, and stopped when he caught the view of his hot tub. His tub was made for six, damn it, not eight. It had never held more than two at one time. Eight teens were leaning back having a grand old time as Shari dished up hot dogs, burgers, and chips to the kids—those who were not hopping in and out between the teens.

"I thought I told you boys to stay away."

"Oh, hey, Uncle E. How're you doing?" Karlton said.

Evidently this little romp with the girls had kept

the boys from racing earlier. "I'd be a lot better if you weren't here." Emmanuel was tired after working all day. Chasing hormonal teens for the rest of the night wasn't ideal entertainment. He glanced at his watch. "You've got one hour. Then you're out of here."

"Uncle Emmanuel!" Karl started.

"Any complaints, you leave right now," he said, climbing onto the deck and making his way to Shari who was dishing a burger to his nephew and his friend. As if the kids weren't a handful, they'd brought their friends with them.

"How's the case going?" Karlton asked.

"You know I can't talk about that while it's going on. But I don't want you guys thinking you can give me help. Just keep your eyes open."

"I saw Mr. Rhodes in Richmond yesterday."

"Where?"

"At Westend Shopping Center." He jumped when Monica elbowed him in the side. "Ouch!"

"Why didn't you tell me you were going to Richmond?" Monica asked Karlton. "I could have gone shopping."

Karlton dunked her under the water. She screamed and came up splashing.

Emmanuel sighed. "Was he alone?" he interrupted.

Karlton caught Monica's flaying hands and glanced up at Emmanuel, grinning. "No, he had that woman who was at the funeral with him."

Emmanuel shook his head. At least he was still in the vicinity. Trevor and Tylan, Jr., came charging by, knocking into him.

"Excuse us," they shouted.

"How much sweets have they had?" Emmanuel asked Shari, as if *she'd* plied the kids with candy and cookies. He hadn't bought sweets when he made his grocery list. "Did they bring their own over?"

She shrugged. "I didn't check their bags. Hungry?"

"Starved." He came over and kissed her lightly. Somebody must have won the race because suddenly all the kids were on the deck, surrounding them.

"Yuck," Chantel said.

"Old folks are always kissing," Phyllis said, grabbing a hot dog from the table.

Shari patted her hand. "Not until you wash your hands," she said.

The girl pulled her hand away from the plate. "My folks are always kissing. They're making babies."

"Where did you get that from?" Emmanuel asked. He was a long way from babies.

"That's not how babies get made," Anthony, Emmanuel's all knowing fourteen-year-old nephew, scoffed at her.

"Yes it is!" she told them as if they should know. "My friend says when your parents want babies, they kiss a lot. She should know. Her mom just had one. Mine should be having babies anytime now. They kiss all the time."

"Who wants to talk about babies?" Tylan, Jr. said, and went in a wild dash with Trevor around the house.

He heard giggles from the Jacuzzi.

"I'm not having any babies," Emmanuel assured Phyllis.

"Well, you'd better stop kissing then, 'cause if you keep it up, you're gonna have some."

She was so serious, Emmanuel smothered a laugh. "Thanks for the warning. I'll take that under advisement."

"Okay." Now that she'd dispensed her advice, she ran into the house to wash up.

"I'll, ah . . . I'll fix you sandwiches . . . while you change," Shari intervened.

"Thanks." Emmanuel went inside to his room to change, listening to the splashes in the Jacuzzi. *The hot tub sure would feel real good about now,* he thought as he dragged his clothing off and changed into shorts. He chuckled. Babies from kissing. Did he think that when he was a kid?

Babies. Shari probably wanted a few. He had to admit that Phyllis was a cute one. But having them underfoot constantly was another matter entirely. He smiled. He might not be ready for them, but he sure liked the process of making them.

At midnight Emmanuel sent the boys on their way. Shari left at the same time, Karlton promising to see her safely home. As much as the boy wore on Emmanuel, he did have a streak of maturity that impressed him. Most eighteen-year-olds thought of sex, cars, and Sega Genesis.

The kids didn't go to bed, however. The girls had pillow fights, talked, tied his phone up with the Internet, and called friends. The older girls experimented with make-up under the younger kids' watchful eye. When Kara and Monica went outside to the Jacuzzi again, Phyllis, Chantel, and Terri experimented with the make-up that had been left on the sink. The boys wore themselves out laughing.

His nephews had lightning bug contests and had so much fun, the younger girls joined them. They ate every hour. At two, Emmanuel finally locked the doors, commanded that no one leave the house, and threatened anyone who spoke above a whisper. Finally he hauled himself off to bed. The kids were still giggling and doing whatever in the other rooms when he fell asleep.

When he awakened the next morning, he found hair dye boxes in the trash can, and nail polish bottles, foot massage containers, and facial stuff on the countertops. It took him immediately back to childhood when he couldn't find a clean space because of Johanna and Pam's junk. Well at least it wasn't in his private bath. They all knew it was off-limits. A man should be able to go into his own bathroom in peace.

By the time he showered, Shari was back to help with breakfast.

"We may as well enjoy a cup of coffee on the deck. They just fell asleep a couple of hours ago."

Shari yawned. "I guess they won't make Sunday School today." Nottoway Baptist preached two Sundays a month. The other two Sundays, they had Sunday school. This wasn't a preaching Sunday.

"What kept you so late yesterday?" Shari asked.

"Howard's out of town. Haven't heard from him for a few days. It's not a cut-and-dried case, for sure. My gut instinct still points to Howard. But there's no proof—yet. He has an alibi."

"He could have paid someone to give it."

Emmanuel nodded. "He could have, but in most of these cases the spouse does the killing. No witnesses, no one to blackmail him later. If he did it, why would he take a chance on someone seeing him move Claudia's body?"

"There must be something for you to hold him on. He shouldn't be running around after murdering his wife."

"We can't arrest a person without evidence. And so far, there isn't any pointing to him."

The stillness of the morning was so unlike the evening before, it took Emmanuel a moment to relax. He could almost forget the kids were even here, if it weren't for the go-carts and toys strewn across the lawn. Farther down the shore he spotted three deer drinking from the river.

"Look," he whispered to Shari, and he urged her up. They walked to the edge of the deck and leaned over the railing to watch as mother, father, and fawn drank their fill. They heard a car drive up and the deer started and disappeared into the trees.

Emmanuel walked to the front of the house where he spotted Luke and Mrs. Drucilla exiting a Lincoln.

"Hey there, Emmanuel," Mrs. Drucilla said when she saw him.

"How are you, Mrs. Drucilla, Luke?"

"We're fine," Luke said.

"Came by to get Chantel, and Tylan, Jr. We're driving up to my daughter's place to stay a couple of days."

"We were supposed to stay a week, but Drucilla don't like to spend much time from home."

"I plan to pick my kale Wednesday morning. Weather's holding up pretty good, but if I let it grow too long, it gets tough."

"Clarice told you she'd pick it for you."

"Tylan married a good girl. She's always helping.

As hard as she works, I don't like bothering her with my stuff." She glanced around. "You got nice, rich land, Emmanuel. Make for a good garden."

Emmanuel never thought about making his own garden. It didn't seem worth the effort for one person. "I guess it would," he responded.

"With those Republicans in office, you're gonna need to save everywhere you can. Things gonna get tight. With a garden, you won't go hungry. I had Luke plow up an extra half acre this year."

"Drucilla, you're going to have to give most of that food away like you always do."

"You don't believe nothing, Luke, but I'm telling you, hard times are coming."

"All right, sweetheart." Luke shook his head. He'd been married long enough to just go along to get along. "I'll plow as much garden space as you want."

Emmanuel always thought they were a cute couple. Mrs. Drucilla was a no-nonsense woman who had come through some tough times—the Depression and the loss of her husband. When her husband died, her brother was about to lose his farm and so was Mrs. Drucilla. Her brother started a whiskey still and became renowned for the quality of his brew. It saved both of them from poverty and it paid for the educations of Mrs. Drucilla's three children. She wasn't a wasteful woman, and she believed in taking care of her own. Nobody held it against her for making illegal whiskey.

Shari joined them and everyone exchanged greetings. "Everyone loved your corn pudding," she said. "I washed out your pan. I'll get it and get the kids." Shari left for the house.

"Come on to the deck and have coffee," Emmanuel said. "Can I get you breakfast?"

"We ate hours ago," Mrs. Drucilla said, "but I'll take a good cup of coffee."

Emmanuel opened the door to his usually neat great room. It now looked like a storm blew through.

"Lordy, they tore up your place. I'm gonna get them up right now and make 'em fix it up."

Tylan, Jr., stirred within his sleeping bag. "Hi, Grandma, Grandpa."

"Hey, there. Did you mind Emmanuel and Shari?" Mrs. Drucilla asked.

"Yeah, Grandma. We were good," Tylan, Jr., said. "We didn't shame the family name."

"Well, it don't look good with this mess round here."

"It's not ours," the boy said.

"Hi, Grandma, Grandpa," Chantel said through the slats of the loft railing.

"Hey, sweetie. You get on up there and get ready so you can visit your grandfolks." Mrs. Drucilla was their great-grandmother.

"Okay," the kids said. Chantel marched to the bathroom in the loft and Tylan, Jr., to the downstairs powder room.

"I'll fix your coffee while you relax on deck," Shari said. She started for the kitchen, but Mrs. Drucilla got all the kids out of bed to clean.

Early Monday morning, Emmanuel got a search warrant for Walter's car. He and Gardell vacuumed every inch and inspected the vehicle for blood or anything unusual. Walter kept a clean vehicle, but under a microscope small details could reveal damning details. Emmanuel used tweezers to collect a couple of short strands of hair from the console.

"Claudia has never been in my car," Walter said emphatically as they collected evidence.

"We're just following procedure. If she hasn't been here, then the evidence will prove that."

"How can it be?"

"You tell us."

Walter tightened his lips and looked on angrily as they invaded his space.

When they finished, Emmanuel drove directly to Richmond to have the contents evaluated. The office was really busy. After he'd waited a couple of hours, he asked the forensics specialist to call him with the findings.

Shari left to head to Gerald's office in hopes that he had no clients. It was still hot as Hades outside. If they didn't get rain soon, the corn would wilt on the stalks, Shari thought as she passed a cornfield. One of the neighbors had seen Emmanuel and Gardell search Walter's car and the news had quickly spread around town.

Gerald's secretary had left for the day, but Gerald was at his desk, sipping coffee and working at his computer.

"Well," he said when he saw her. Then he blinked. "To what do I owe the pleasure of this visit?"

"I wanted to talk to you," Shari said as she went to the fridge for a bottle of water.

He smiled. "I'm always available for you."

Always open to the baby, she thought as she took a seat and placed her clutch on her lap.

He continued to stare at her with a smile on his face.

"Oh, for goodness' sake. Say it, and get it off your chest."

"I'm just surprised, that's all. You're dressed more like you did in high school and college. I guess I don't need to ask why." But then he frowned.

Emmanuel again. Nobody was good enough for baby sister. "Let's skip Emmanuel. I'm here to talk about Walter," she said.

His brows drew together. "You know I don't discuss clients. Not even with family."

"Do you think he could have murdered Claudia?"

He narrowed his eyes as an angry tinge covered his face. "He hasn't been charged with anything, and he won't be convicted."

"I'm not talking about conviction. I'm asking if you think he could have hurt her. They searched his car today."

"Shari, you know I can't discuss his case with you. You know the rules."

"So you don't care that you may be protecting a man who could do this again? That the citizens of Nottoway may be in danger because of him?"

His eyes grew as cold as an artic winter. "Be careful of name-calling. Shari, I realize that you're working closely with the Women's Center, but the accused still need representation. This case is none of your business, but I don't believe he murdered Claudia."

She hated when people sought protection behind excuses or rules. "I'll tell you what is my business.

The fact that he's walking around free to rape me or any woman."

"And if he's innocent? Why should he be made a scapegoat? You're not the judge and jury. All the evidence isn't in yet. That's all I'm going to say about this case." He turned away from her. "I've got work to do. I'm disappointed, Shari. I thought you were above that."

Shari pounced out of her seat and leaned over the desk. "I'm not above protecting innocents who are raped every year."

He stood with his hands balled on the desk. "Does that mean an innocent man should be convicted for a crime he didn't commit? Walter isn't a statistic. He's an individual who deserves the best defense that he can get."

Gerald didn't understand. He was a man, after all. How would he understand? She turned and stomped out of Gerald's office, running smack into Walter at the door of the outer office.

He reached up and caught her arms with his hands. She quailed at his touch.

"Shari?" he whispered. When she didn't respond, she saw the disappointment in his eyes before his face tensed in embarrassment and anger.

To Shari, he looked tired and worn-out, even sicker than he'd looked at the office. He was Gerald's client and she was in her brother's place of business. She didn't know what she felt—hadn't had time to adjust. She stood mute, gazing at him.

Finally his hands dropped from her arms. He stepped to the side, passed her, and strode toward Gerald's office.

For a moment, her feet felt rooted to the spot.

Finally she turned and looked at him. Gerald shook Walter's hand, and offered him a seat. Then he came to the door, gave her a stern look, and closed the door behind her.

Shari turned and left, going out into the heat of the day. Somehow she felt like she'd let them down.

Walter and Gerald.

Chapter 12

Tuesday morning, Emmanuel got a call from the lab in Richmond. The two short strands of hair found in Walter's car were pubic hair and the blood from inside the trunk was Claudia's. Any other evidence had been wiped away. Soon after, Walter was arrested for Claudia's murder.

Emmanuel remembered collecting the hair from the center console. There hadn't been any dents or breakage to indicate a struggle. Sex in the console area would be difficult, and he kept wondering why he didn't find semen or something else on seats that obviously hadn't been cleaned in months, or any other evidence that proved Claudia had been there.

It seemed almost too perfect. Where was the motive? Walter had been pining for Claudia for months. As soon as she freed herself from a husband who didn't love her, didn't care about her, her true love killed her. It didn't make sense. Something in Emmanuel's gut told him that he had the wrong person, but he couldn't make arrests on gut instinct.

Walter's file disclosed that Walter's brother had been in and out of trouble since high school, but Walter's record was spotless. He'd been a stellar student, included in honor societies—not that the honor society made him an honest man. But he had no criminal record. He'd gone to college on a full scholarship. He'd graduated magna cum laude, worked summer jobs, received a graduate scholarship, and completed it with high honors. There was no money in the family.

After that he'd worked in New York for a while. A year ago, Jonathan had recruited him for a special project at Blake Industries. Walter contributed regularly to his pension plan. He saved ten percent of every paycheck. He sent payments to his mother from each paycheck. He attended church regularly. His life was as clean as a whistle. Nothing to point to any criminal activity.

On the other hand there was Howard, with no foreseeable evidence against him but who had every reason to kill his wife.

Where did that leave the investigation? A puzzle yet to be completed. Emmanuel loathed half finished puzzles.

Emmanuel shut the file. It was four. Shari returned to work today ahead of schedule because of Walter's problems. Both of them couldn't be absent. He'd fix dinner for her and try to convince her to stay the night.

* * *

The easiest meal to cook, Emmanuel thought as he dropped a couple of steaks in the grocery cart, was steak, potatoes, and a salad he'd mixed together at the salad bar. He'd fire up the grill and slap the steaks and potatoes on it. Not very imaginative, but tasty, especially with the smoky grilled flavor.

He hoped he could talk Shari into leaving work at a reasonable hour. Imagining Shari in the Jacuzzi in the bathroom covered in bubbles sent thrills up his spine. They could skip dinner and feast on each other. His groin heated at the thought of plunging deeply into her again. *Damn.* Emmanuel reached for the cell phone and punched in Shari's office number. She didn't answer. Probably in a meeting, he thought, disappointed. He left a message and headed for home.

He'd driven three miles before he tried Shari's home phone. She answered on the second ring.

"I've got steaks waiting for you."

"Who's cooking?" There was a suspicious tone to her voice, like he was just another man waiting for a woman to come home and wait hand and foot on him. His mom always had dinner waiting when Dad rolled in, but she'd always worked at home. He knew better than to expect that from today's woman. He only had to watch Johanna. Besides, Shari's cooking skills weren't what drove him at the moment.

"Yours truly. Meet me at my house in a half hour," he said, finding it difficult to wait much longer. He hoped his need didn't frighten her.

"Okay."

"Just like that?" There had to be a catch for her to acquiesce that quickly.

There was a tight edge to her voice. "Sure," she said, again surprising Emmanuel.

"Is anything wrong?"

"You arrested Walter today."

Damn the grapevine. "I was going to tell you about that later."

She sighed. "I don't want to talk about it right now. Let's just enjoy the evening."

He could almost hear the wheels turning in her head. "All right. Tomorrow is soon enough," he said. "Get there as soon as you can."

Emmanuel made it home in ten minutes. He made a marinade for the steaks and stuck them in the refrigerator along with a bottle of wine. Then he showered before Shari arrived.

Shari was tired of thinking about Walter, and about her fears. She wanted to relax for one night.

When Emmanuel saw her, he said, "Let's get into the Jacuzzi."

"I forgot to bring a bathing suit."

His smile was dead serious. "You won't need one."

"We're using the inside one?"

"If it'll make you feel better, although it's nice to look at the sky on a clear night."

Shari hesitated. "Okay." Why not run on the wild side for a change?

He got her a beach towel and she went into his bedroom to disrobe. She came out wearing only the towel. Emmanuel tried very hard not to let his mind center on getting her in bed. Emmanuel went to his room, took off his clothes and wrapped a towel around his waist. He hid a couple of prophylactics near the Jacuzzi. He turned on the music that was softly piped outside. The mood was romantic and seductive as they climbed into the hot tub together, shucking the towels as he turned on the jets.

Emmanuel sank into the water, letting the water sluice over his skin and the jets massage his muscles, erasing the tension. He drew Shari close to him. She lay her head back on his arm as she gazed at the sky. A peaceful heaven dotted with brightly lit stars. In this isolated spot one could almost believe that they were alone in the world. They both relaxed quietly for a while letting the trials of the day drain from them.

Many long minutes passed before they spoke and pointed out stars in the night sky to each other, but with a naked woman sitting by him in the Jacuzzi, Emmanuel wasn't thinking about stars, shapes, planets, comets or the full moon.

With Shari's warm body pressed against his and the water undulating against breasts that he longed to explore, his erection grew harder and hot under the pulsing water. He moved his hand up her arm and pressed his lips to the graceful column of her neck. Her skin was smooth and hot and drove Emmanuel wild with a feverish need that threatened to consume him. Enjoying the texture of her soft skin, Emmanuel moved his hand to cup her breast, stoking gently, loving the difference that made her so fascinating and irresistible. For a fleeting moment he thought how wonderful it would be to come home to this every night.

Watching the slowly whirling stars overhead, Shari yearned to become part of Emmanuel. She felt as though she was floating in a magical, mystical world of spiraling stars and enchanted planets.

She slid her arms around his firm, slippery waist, gliding her hands to his sinewy thighs. His manhood pulsed when her arm brushed lightly against him. Placing her hand around him she caressed him gently. With great eagerness she let herself slide into the magnetism of his tempting mouth. Her body vibrated with need and wanting. At this instant, she'd never wanted a man more than she wanted Emmanuel.

His kisses grew insistent and demanding. He stood and dragged her out of the water, grasping the towels and laying both onto the deck. The air chilled her hot skin. He urged her down and rested on his knees beside her. The chill was just a memory as with blatant hunger his eyes glided over her damp skin from her head to her toes, lingering at her breasts and her thick thatch of hair. He gazed at her as if he were starved for the sight of her. Her heart beat furiously.

He lowered himself to her and grasped a nipple gently between his lips.

"Do you know how long I've wanted you?" His warm breath whispered against her skin. "I've been going out of my mind, counting the seconds when I can be with you again."

She smoothed a shaky hand across the wide breadth of his shoulders. "About as much as I've wanted to be with you."

His groan was deep and feral as he came up to kiss her urgently, stroke her persistently.

"Oh, yes . . ." she moaned when he suckled on her breasts again. She only wanted him inside her, surrounding her. But he took his time, pleasuring every inch of her body and she his, before she finally slid the condom on him and he pushed into her, giving her the release she desired. They moved slowly at first as if to savor the pleasure but soon the pace increased, and the beat of their pulses matched the pulsing of the water jets as they climbed to the stars and fell like a spiral into an oblivion of ecstasy. As their heartbeats slowed, Shari wondered if it was the magic of the stars that had driven them to this mysterious enchanting fantasy, or moved her to whisper, "I love you, Emmanuel."

Shari spent a restless night beside Emmanuel. At six while he was still sleeping, she slipped away to her home to dress for work. Two things bothered her. The first was that she'd told Emmanuel that she loved him and he had never acknowledged her confession—not that he cared deeply for her, especially not that he loved her. She didn't want to think of the implication of his evading her statement.

The second thing that bothered her was her response to Walter. She took pride in fairness. Some nagging doubt told her that she'd been unfair to him. Through her healing process she realized that not all men were rapists, but she still had to be on her guard. Computers were the only similarities between Walter and Simon. Simon had been obnoxious and difficult to work with. He boasted that he only gave women what they wanted. Her sense of justice for women warred very hard with grudging empathy for Walter. Walter was solicitous, always helping when it was needed. He didn't have a problem with a female supervisor, while Simon loathed having one. He'd thought that by raping her he was putting her in her place.

She was torn between trusting and not trusting. Where should she draw the line with trusting and believing? She knew that most men would say anything to get in your pants, but that not all of them would rape to get there.

She wasn't naïve enough to believe anyone could tell a rapist by looks or occupation, but accepting her past meant that she would sometimes have to go by nothing more than gut instinct. She didn't have to embrace Walter, but she was well aware that many innocent people were convicted of crimes they didn't commit. Not everyone had a handy alibi—especially when they lived alone.

When Shari reached her home, the answering machine was beeping. She retrieved her messages. Two were from Walter. He wanted to talk to her. She returned his call, and he asked if she would meet him for breakfast at Johanna's restaurant.

After she showered and dressed for work, she drove directly to Johanna's. As she walked into the hotel, vacationers dressed in shorts and tank tops, and businesswomen and men in lightweight suits started to the dining room. Walter was already waiting for her at a table in a quiet corner. As Shari walked across the carpeted floor to join him, she didn't have a clue of what she'd say to him .

He wore a suit and tie, throwing the meeting immediately to business. He stood when she reached the table.

"Thank you for meeting me here," he said stiffly, but he held his head high and his shoulders straight.

Shari took the chair across from him. A waitress

brought coffee, left a menu for her, and quickly scuttled away.

"Have you ordered yet?" Shari asked him. In her peripheral vision she could see people reading the *Nottoway Review* and looking their way. Shari had already glimpsed the front-page article that featured Walter as the murderer. She knew he hated being in a public place right now.

"No. I waited for you."

Shari nodded and perused the menu. Her mind was more on how she would handle the situation than it was on food. She was a manager. She couldn't bring her personal feelings into business associations. When the waitress returned, she ordered a ham-and-cheese omelet and wondered how she'd eat it all. Walter ordered toast and a poached egg. She doubted that he'd eat even that small amount. The waitress quickly left again and Shari added sugar and cream to her coffee. As she tasted it, she got her first jump start on her day.

"I know that it will be uncomfortable for me to return to work right now—for the employees as well as myself. I was wondering if you would let me work on my computer from home."

Shari opened her mouth to respond, but before she could, Walter continued.

"I need to stay busy right now, and I need the income. I know it wouldn't do any good to protest that I'm innocent, and that people won't believe me if I do say so until the real murderer is found—if he's found." His hand was closed tightly around his coffee cup. Again she was struck by how differently from Simon he reacted. Simon was always calm, even in the face of opposition. She'd been incredulous at the man's gall.

Shari was silent for a moment, trying to remember that a person was innocent until proven guilty. Walter was not in custody whether he worked or not, so what harm could it do for him to work from home?

She found herself nodding. "That will be fine."

She'd worked companionably by this man for a year. Some things were simply best left for God to answer. She wasn't omniscient. She had no answers, so she found herself conversing with Walter as if nothing had happened. She talked about inane subjects to relax him, and it worked to a certain extent. The other patrons in the restaurant continued to stare at them. Walter didn't look at anyone but at her. She ate only half of her omelet. He barely touched his egg and toast.

Shari made it to the office around nine. When she went in search of Kara, she passed the computer room and noticed several summer interns crowded around a computer. She put her things on her desk in her office, and went back to the computer room to speak to the interns, but they were really engrossed in some program.

"Hello," Shari said. "What're you working on?" She edged closer.

"Just some program," Kara said, but continued to watch the screen.

"What program?"

The kids looked sheepishly at her.

"Just some security retrieval program we were practicing on," Kara said.

The interns relaxed somewhat as Kara did all the talking. She was the owner's niece, after all. They obviously felt she could get away with things they couldn't.

"Don't let me stop you."

"It's snoop software. We were checking out how it can retrieve erased mail messages."

Shari watched as Kara demonstrated the software. Then Shari frowned. She'd seen some software with that name when she was retrieving mail messages on Claudia's computer.

She got the kids to erase a program and retrieve it with the retrieval CD. Then she asked for a copy of it and went into her office and called Emmanuel. She was told that he'd gone to Richmond and wouldn't be back for a couple of hours. Phoenix wasn't in, either, so Shari left a message for Emmanuel to call her.

When the phone rang a couple of hours later, it was Emmanuel.

"I need to look at Claudia's computer again. There may be something I missed before," she said.

"Can you come now?" he asked.

"I'll be there in twenty minutes." Shari grabbed her purse, shut down her computer, and left the office.

She was still apprehensive about her declaration of love last night. Even on the phone, Emmanuel hadn't said a word about that. Did he plan to ignore it forever?

When she arrived at the sheriff's office, Emmanuel had already hooked up the computer for her. She sat down and worked with the program the kids had given her. Sure enough there was snoop software.

"This means that someone was snooping on her e-mail messages. She wouldn't have needed the snoop software if she was the only user. Either she thought someone had used her computer, or someone was spying on *her*."

Gardell stuck his head in the door. "Howard's on the run."

"He went to work earlier today."

"But he never returned. We can't find him anywhere. I've got an APB out on him."

A reporter lurked around the office and Emmanuel was so busy getting rid of him that Shari didn't have time to talk privately with him. After she demonstrated the software, she left for the office. Undoubtedly Walter was no longer a suspect, but Shari would let her brother break the good news to him.

That evening, Emmanuel went to his parent's home, otherwise he'd have spent half the night tossing and turning. Might as well work, making himself so tired he'd have no option but to fall into a deep sleep. Jonathan and James, Pam's husband, had already begun the basement project. The kids were playing in the yard. The wives were on the screened porch snacking and arguing. Jonathan wasn't around to curb Johanna. Emmanuel heard them and edged in the opposite direction, but before he made it to the basement door, Pam had intervened, putting an end to the bickering.

Emmanuel found all the men in the basement nailing up sheetrock.

"There's an extra nail gun over there," James said,

pointing to an area near the stairs. Emmanuel retrieved it and shot nails into one end of the sheetrock while Jonathan nailed the other end.

"Good to see you, son. You've been scarce lately," his dad said. He didn't work very often with them, but now that he was retired, he had more time.

"What are you doing down here?" Emmanuel asked.

"Better than sparring with the women."

Emmanuel wasn't the only coward in the bunch. He realized that working in the basement was taking the easy way out—for now. Eventually he'd have to deal with Shari, but right now, he wasn't ready to confront her declaration of love. Besides, he wasn't so sure that she really loved him. They'd spent so little time together. How could he tell? Their relationship was her first attempt at real intimacy since the rape. Her reaction could be a rebound. He was afraid that her feelings for him were just gratitude. She'd come to her senses and then where would he be?

He thought of Jonathan who seemed pleased with his marriage to Johanna. Emmanuel didn't see how he could stand living in the same house with her. He could never put up with a wife like Johanna.

Shari was nothing like her though, so he didn't have that excuse.

"I'll be right back guys," his dad said.

The men put the nail gun down and took a water break. Both seemed satisfied with their choices— even his dad. As much as he loved his mom, he couldn't see himself married to a woman like her, either.

"What is it, Emmanuel? Seems like you've got the

weight of the world on your shoulders," Jonathan said.

"Just thinking."

"About what?" asked James.

"Women. What else?"

Both men grinned.

"Oh that."

"He's been bitten by the bug," James said.

"I just don't see how you could stand being married. How can you give up your peace?"

Jonathan threw him a bottle of water out of the cooler. "There are advantages to settling with the right woman."

James grinned. "You can say that again."

Emmanuel took a swig from his bottle. "There's more to dealing with them than sex. I don't know how you put up with Johanna's mouth."

"Hey man, that's my wife you're talking about. She's not so bad."

"What do you do? Stuff cotton in your ears?"

"I want to hear every word she says."

"Jokes aside, how did you know she was the right one?"

"You'll know. When life without her is pure misery."

James nodded. "It's that simple."

That was no answer. He'd been miserable plenty of times. Misery didn't prompt him toward marriage. He was facing a couple of fools who didn't know what they were talking about. Still, they were married and they seemed happy. He wasn't. But he wasn't quite miserable either. But then he still had Shari. The question was, where did they go from here?

* * *

The next morning Shari read the article in the paper about her involvement in the murder investigation and about the roses Walter planted at the head of Claudia's grave. The article cast an eerie light on Walter's obsession, but the reporter had interviewed several women who thought his romantic, tender gesture was touching.

Walter must have loved Claudia very much, Shari realized. It would take a while for the cloud of doubt to settle. She left a message for him on his answering machine. He'd called her office saying he'd be on vacation for the rest of the week. She planned to visit him after work and called him to tell him she was coming by. He still hadn't answered his phone, so Shari drove directly to Emmanuel's. In the last few weeks a day hadn't gone by that Emmanuel didn't call. Suddenly he was avoiding her. She knew the end was near. There was no reason for her to torture herself about them. For him there was no "them," and there was no reason for her to keep waiting for a call that wasn't coming.

Saying she loved him had changed everything. Had she kept her feelings to herself, things could go on as they were. But now that she'd acknowledged it, they couldn't go back to the way it was before.

She'd be uncomfortable. She'd be anticipating the breakup. She'd make him uncomfortable.

By blurting out her feelings, she'd messed up a perfectly good relationship that could have gone on as it was until it died a natural death.

He'd refused to deal with her declarations, leaving her with two choices. She could confront him or she could continue on as if she'd never uttered the words. She couldn't ignore what she'd said. She wasn't one to avoid an issue. They needed to deal with her feelings. They couldn't go on as though it hadn't happened. Shari had thought she could handle an affair, no matter how long it lasted, expect it to go nowhere, and be satisfied. *Live with the here and now.* But she'd never been a here-and-now woman. Her sights were always fixed on the future and what it would entail. She couldn't continue with Emmanuel and get her heart entangled with him more than it already was, only for him to say adios in a couple of months. It was better to end it all now when she could come out of it with only half a crack in her heart. The future was a foregone conclusion. Emmanuel wasn't a staying kind of man. The dilemma she found herself in wasn't his fault. The blame lay totally at her feet. She knew what he was capable of offering from the very beginning. It was she who'd changed—not him.

Emmanuel was leaving the house as she walked toward the front door. His smile when he saw her turned guarded.

"Hi," he said.

She'd grown to love his peaceful hideaway. She'd miss it, as much as she'd miss him. "We need to discuss a few things, Emmanuel."

He glanced at his watch with a weary sigh. "Shari, I don't have the time right now."

"I'll make it short."

He hesitated for only a second. "Okay," he said, and backed into the house, holding the door for her to enter.

"Tuesday night I told you that I loved you, and you never responded."

Panic edged around Emmanuel's thoughts. "What do you want from me?" he asked, as if he were far from ready for this discussion.

"I want to know how you feel about me."

"Shari, I like you—a lot."

Shari was startled. Even though she knew forever wasn't in his lifestyle, she loved this man, and he only *liked* her? Somehow, she expected more than that. How did he feel that he could offer so little? "That's all you have to say?" she asked, bleakness in her voice.

Emmanuel broke out in a cold sweat. He knew she wanted him to say that he was ready for babies and forever. True, he thought he'd wanted a serious relationship, but he wasn't ready to marry, to lose his freedom. He wasn't ready to give her up, either. Tuesday night was the best loving he'd ever had.

"We need more time to think this through," he said. He knew he was stalling, but what more could he do? Why couldn't she just accept the joy they brought each other?

The look she sent him was a mixture of sadness and anger. "There isn't much you don't know about me. I've been unfair. In the middle of things I realized I can't live a happy, free-sex life just to slake our lust-ridden urges."

"That's not . . ."

"Of course it is. In a couple of months, maybe six, you'll dump me with some trite words like 'It's just not working out, babe, but it was good while it lasted.'"

"It's not like that at all. You're making what we have sound cheap when, in fact, it's very special. Shari, there are no guarantees in life. We don't know what will happen with us. What we have is good—better than good."

Shari shook her head. "In other words, you aren't ready to commit, but you want to continue to enjoy the sex while the getting's good. On the other hand you're watching the time tick away. Soon after the sex fizzles, it's goodbye, Shari."

"Don't put words in my mouth. I didn't say that."

"You haven't said anything that makes sense. I'm not asking you to love me. My feelings are my problems." she sighed. "If I didn't love you, it would be easier to continue because we'd both be having fun. But I know I couldn't continue the intimacy that went nowhere."

"Shari, you're mixing gratitude with love. You won't feel this way a few months from now." Struggling for solid ground, Emmanuel ran an agitated hand over his head. "What is love anyway? Some ethereal . . ."

"Don't play psychologist with me. I know what I feel. Either you feel it or you don't, and obviously you don't." She gathered up her courage. She didn't want to be so weak that she'd accept anything to keep him. If they continued, that's exactly what she'd end up doing until he was ready to let her go. She might be the youngest in the family, but she had more backbone than that. She caressed his jaw. "Goodbye, Emmanuel. I'm not willing to invest more of my heart in a temporary liaison. I'll make it easy for you. It's over."

"What? Just because I won't fall in line with your little plan?" He swiped the air with his hand. "It's got to be your way or the highway?"

"I want to be with someone who can at least admit

what his feelings are and at least have goals beyond a few months. I'm not asking that you promise to marry me. I don't think this relationship is as serious for you as it is for me. And because of that, yes, it's going to be the highway."

Shari turned and left, a crushing weight hammering into her chest. Yes, she was capable of enjoying a relationship again and she was thankful to Emmanuel for that, but not so thankful that she'd give up her values and beliefs.

Emmanuel had stood numb for several shocked moments before he'd rushed out to the SUV to return to work. Now he sat at his desk unable to get Shari off his mind. He wasn't going to let a woman rush him into making hasty decisions. He slammed the file onto the desk and pushed back his chair. *Women. They always had to screw up a good thing.*

He swore not to let it get him down. The relationship would have ended anyway. It had just ended sooner rather than later this time.

Emmanuel suddenly felt strange as he grabbed his jacket and left the office. A sense of loss permeated him. He liked Shari a lot. It was hard giving her up. But liking her was a long way from love.

He didn't have time to think about this. Right now he had to arrest Howard for murdering Claudia. The pathology report on Claudia's internal organs had finally come back. It had placed Claudia's time of death between midnight and five—well within the time Howard was home. Evidently the body had been chilled and that threw off the time of death. The added info about the computer clinched the deal.

When Emmanuel reached Howard's house, Howard's car was still missing. An APB had been issued. Information had been sent to Richmond where he'd last been seen.

After her trip to see Emmanuel, Shari's mind was reeling, but she still had to apologize to Walter. He had gone through an emotional turmoil that had been much worse. His car was in the yard, so she surmised that he must be home. When she knocked on his door there wasn't a response to her summons. She walked around the back of the house and was about to leave when she spotted him walking from the woods to the house. He carried a bucket and fishing pole in his hand. He wore jean shorts and a T-shirt with ripped-out sleeves, not for style but from wear.

As he neared, she realized he didn't look very hospitable. This was a day for confrontations, she realized as she geared herself up. "Hello," she said when he neared her.

"Did you get my message?" he asked.

She nodded. "I did, but I wanted to talk to you."

"About what?"

"I wanted to apologize." Although she noticed several fish tucked into melting ice in his bucket, just a hint of their odor floated to her nose. At least they were fresh.

"Accepted," he said, and walked on.

Shari fell in step with him. "I wanted to explain some things."

He glanced at her for a speaking moment. Then he leaned the pole against the wall, opened the door, and ushered her inside. He walked to the sink with his bucket while she made herself comfortable at the kitchen table, debating how to start the conversation. Sometimes the truth was easier than tact.

She started at the very beginning—with Simon.

Chapter 13

Weeks later, Emmanuel shoved the covers back, got out of bed, and pulled a beer out the fridge. He ended up on the deck, twisting off the bottle cap, as he looked skyward while he took a long pull on his drink. He hadn't been able to enjoy the view of the night sky without thinking of his last night with Shari. That night had a dreamlike quality. He wondered if the magic of it could ever be repeated, even with Shari, or if it was like a shooting star that burned bright and hot, yet was suddenly extinguished forever.

Even in this deserted stretch of woods, the night wasn't silent. Nature had a song of her own, but her spirited lyrics couldn't keep the deep abiding loss from stripping shreds off Emmanuel's peace.

After all this time, the bed still felt deserted without Shari's warmth beside him. Loneliness consumed him and wouldn't let go. He never had problems living by himself, but now . . . perhaps this was payback for all the women he'd left.

Had he really been so callous as to deserve the brush Shari had painted him with? Had he been that fickle with women's feelings, their needs, their desires? He'd always prided himself on taking great pains to cater to their needs. He never failed in lovemaking. Women never left his bed wanting. But he knew Shari spoke about more than sex and intimacy. She wanted more than he was capable of giving. What they had had been developing beautifully, but she wanted a man's body and soul wrapped up and delivered in a neat little package.

Now the deep sense of loss was worse than the precious space and freedom he guarded. It wasn't the fact that she wasn't here physically that hit him so damn hard, but that she was no longer a part of his life. His feelings for her had pierced a deeper level than any other relationship. But marriage and forever? Could his feelings be . . . ?

Shari felt loads better now that Howard was no longer in the vicinity and the air had been cleared with Walter, although she'd feel a heck of a lot better if Howard was found. Perhaps she could sleep peacefully now—even when she wasn't with Emmanuel. She tried not to go there. As it was, her heart was smarting enough from his absence. Maybe she'd spoken too hastily. No, she hadn't. She'd made the decision that she could live with.

For the first time in weeks, she hung her clothes outside on the clothesline rather than dry them in the dryer. Sometimes she just liked the fresh smell of the out-of-doors—liked to see the clothing flapping in the wind. There was something nostalgic about the image, not to mention the relief on her electric bill when she didn't use the dryer.

Shari glanced at her watch. Mrs. Drucilla's birthday celebration was this afternoon. After this, she'd take her bath so she'd be on time. First there would be a program at church followed by the banquet at the Riverview Restaurant. Since the affair was so large, all the local restaurants were contributing something. Clarice, Karina, Johanna, and other committee members had worked tirelessly on the festivities for months.

Shari glanced above her hat to the sunlight that shone down hot on her as she pinned sheets to the line. She reached into the clothes basket for a another sheet. From the other side of the sheet, she spotted dirty sneakers sticking out. She straightened to see Howard staring at her at eye level.

Panic seized her as she watched his tense features and the secret malice that gleamed from his eyes.

"So you're the nosy woman who don't know how to keep your nose in your own business," he said, and reached for her. "I'm here to teach you a lesson. Teach the next woman who comes against me to think twice before she sticks her nose where it don't belong."

"So you did kill Claudia," Shari said, knowing the truth before he replied.

"Nobody leaves me. Nobody crosses me. You got that? Not Claudia, not you. But you won't be here to tell anybody. I'm giving you some of what I gave her." The menace in his voice was a palpable thing. No trace emerged of the grieving widower who'd sat sedately at church and the gravesite.

Shari sprinted back from him. He outweighed her by at least fifty pounds. Suddenly everything she'd learned from her many self-defense classes flew from her mind. Everything she'd taught other students escaped from her thoughts. Panic lodged in her throat and limbs, along with the nightmare of what had happened to her before.

But as he came for her, she realized this *wasn't* like before. This time she wasn't incapacitated by drugs. She had her wits. She had her skills, and her strength, as long as she kept her wits. And when he grabbed for her, she hollered at the top of her lungs and attacked. Her wild screech startled him, giving her the advantage. The screech alone wouldn't have done it, but he didn't expect her attack.

When he came at her again, she went for his throat, missed, and caught the side of his neck. The strike didn't incapacitate him, but it struck hard enough to hurt. He suddenly bent low and the punch she'd aimed for his groin reached his stomach. He bent even more under the impact, but her strikes only served to enrage him further.

Shari kicked him in the knee and slapped both ears with the palm of her hands. He dropped to the ground, screaming blasphemies, holding one hand to his ear, the other to his knee.

Shari ran into the house and locked her door behind her. Adrenaline ran high. Her heart pounded in her chest. She'd done it, she thought as she headed to the phone, and almost leaped out of her skin when she spotted a gun pointed at her.

"Where is Howard?" the woman behind the gun asked.

"Who are you?" Shari could fight, but she couldn't outrun a bullet. Think of your training! Howard wouldn't be down for long. How was she going to get herself out of this?

The woman waved the gun. "Turn around and unlock the door."

Shari turned slightly and did as the woman ordered. "Who are you? Why are you here?"

"Don't worry about that, Miss Goody Two-Shoes."

"I don't understand how I fit into this."

"You're keeping Howard from his money. If it wasn't for you, the computer guy would have been blamed for Claudia's murder and we'd be rich. Shoulda kept your nose out of things that weren't any of your business."

"We?"

"Yes. Howard and me. We were planning to get married. Now all that's ruined because of you. I ought to shoot you right now, but it's got to look like the serial murderer did you in."

"None of his victims were shot, were they?"

The woman narrowed her eyes. Shari heard someone struggling outside.

"Help!" Howard hollered out. "I need help!"

The woman narrowed her eyes at Shari. "What did you do to him?"

Shari shrugged.

She waved the gun to urge Shari on. "Start walking. Move slowly. No tricks or I'll shoot you. Don't matter to me how you go."

Shari opened the door and walked slowly out. She could handle one. What would she do to protect herself against two people, with one carrying a gun? Howard's rage would give him extra strength and cruelty. She wasn't Trivet or Shaft. She was merely a woman.

Think, Shari, think!

Howard held on to the corner of the house, breathing hard, clutching his gut and his leg. His knee protruded at an odd angle.

"What the hell happened to you?" the woman asked.

The malevolence in the gaze he pointed at Shari frightened her. "She . . . You be careful around her," he gasped.

"You can't do anything right," the woman said. "I've always got to think for you and clean up your messes. Come on," she said to Shari. "You're going to transfer the money from your savings account to checking using your computer. Computer geeks do everything on computers."

"So I'll give you my money and then you'll kill me. How dumb do you think I am?" Shari asked.

"You be real good and we might let you live."

Yeah, right, Shari thought.

The woman edged the gun closer to Shari. Howard's face was strained with pain.

"Go to the car. I've got her checkbooks." the woman told Howard. "I can handle her."

Now Shari was sandwiched between the two of them. Fear roared so loud in her ears, she heard a horn toot. As she watched, the woman turned her attention from Shari and Shari kicked her hard. The gun went flying across the ground. The three of them dived for it as one. Shari hadn't been torturing herself with exercise for nothing. This was a live-or-die situation. She got to the gun, rolled, and pointed it at the woman as she began to close the distance between them.

"Back up!" Shari shouted.

The woman stopped at the warning Shari flashed. Shari heard a car door slam and someone approaching, but she kept her eyes firmly focused on the two before her.

"Who is it?" she called out as the footsteps neared.

"Karlton. My mom sent me. . . ." He stopped when he took in the scene. "Oh, shit."

"Go call the police," she told him. When he started to skirt them, she said, "Go through the front."

As he went into the house and Shari gazed at Howard and the woman, she felt a certain satisfaction that she was able to take care of herself this time. That all her training had been for something. She'd add that to her next class. Perhaps more women would take a self-defense class. She wasn't a fool. She realized that she was handed a stroke of luck with Karlton's visit. Her limbs trembled so hard, the gun shook like an oak in high wind. But she was still here, unscathed, and behind the safety of a gun.

The woman was Saffron Jackson. She and Howard had been taken away, and most of the officers and Karlton had left. Emmanuel lingered.

As soon as the front door to the house slammed shut, he gathered Shari close to him and kissed her deeply and urgently, forgetting that they'd just broken up. That little fact was insignificant in the face of the recent danger.

"The drive from the station to here was the longest

of my life. I've never known fear like that before,'' he said, his voice hoarse and strained against her lips. He kissed her again, her sweet aroma intoxicating him. "I don't know what I would have done without you."

"I'm okay. Really." His arms around her were a soothing balm, and she caressed his back, leaning her head against his supportive chest. His strong heartbeat comforted her like a lullaby.

He leaned back to look at her closely, ran a hand down her arms, her back, pressed her back to him. "Are you sure?"

She nodded. She still trembled from the experience and her insides wouldn't settle down.

"Well, *I'm* not okay."

She laughed and their laughter served to break the tension.

"Hey, Emmanuel!" Someone pounded on the door. "Let's go."

"Dammit." Emmanuel sighed. "We're always getting interrupted. I'm stopping by tonight."

"I won't be here." She untangled herself from him and stepped back. Emmanuel grasped her hands as if he couldn't completely let her go. "I'll be at Mrs. Drucilla's birthday party. And I think it's best that we stay away from each other. Thank you, for being here."

"Shari . . ."

"Let's go!" someone shouted again.

"I'm coming," he called through the door.

Shari tugged her hands free. "*Just go*. I'm fine now."

He started to say something else but the knock

wouldn't let up. "I've got to get to the station. We always get interrupted at the most important times."

Howard's capture had been the main topic of conversation at Mrs. Drucilla's ninetieth birthday celebration at church and the restaurant. Howard's mother's absence had been noticeable because she'd been part of the program. No one in his family attended. Gladys Jones had taken center stage in her place. At the program's planning, she'd been miffed anyway because she hadn't gotten the coveted part. Now she felt vindicated.

Shari felt like the fifth wheel at the reception. It seemed everyone was paired off except her.

All in all, the festivities had been grand, she thought. Mrs. Drucilla and Luke were beside themselves with joy.

She watched Phoenix finish a dance with Kara. Father and daughter. Then the two of them approached Karlton and Karl. Phoenix laughed at a joke one of the boys made. The triplets talked among themselves while Phoenix looked on, his expression nostalgic. The triplets were leaving for college in a couple of weeks and Shari knew he'd miss them terribly. But before they left, they'd probably drive him crazy. The three left him to dance with their dates and Phoenix approached Shari.

"How are you holding up?" he asked her. The last time he came through, the line had been long.

"Couldn't be better."

"There's something to be said for those self-defense classes. Anytime you need help, let me know. I'll make sure you get what you need."

"Thank you," Shari said. Several ladies had spoken to her today about starting another class. Phoenix joined his wife who had kept a close eye on the festivities even though she'd scheduled extra staff. The restaurant was her baby.

Gladys Jones came toward her. Shari got the feeling that Emmanuel's mom never really liked her.

"I haven't seen much of you lately," Mrs. Jones said. "I hope you can make it to the family dinner next Sunday. Usually the entire family attends."

Hadn't Emmanuel told his family that they were through? "Thank you for inviting me, but . . ."

"We'd love to have you." This was not an invitation, but a command.

The band announced the last song then began to play "Save the Last Dance for Me." Shari saw Karlton approach her.

"How are you, Mrs. Jones?"

"Doing well, Karlton. Be sure to leave me your address and I'll mail food to you when you're at college. I know you love to eat." Mrs. Jones had babysat the triplets when they were young and she considered them part of her family.

"Oh, thank you, Mrs. Jones. We'll look forward to it. I want to steal Shari for this dance."

"Go ahead. You all have your fun."

As Karlton led Shari to the dance floor, she noticed Gladys' husband walking in her direction.

Karlton gathered her in a respectable embrace and Shari couldn't help wishing that she were in Emmanuel's arms. As if she had conjured him up with her thoughts, he appeared at Karlton's shoulder and tapped it.

"I hope you've saved the last dance for me," he said to Shari even though he stood next to Karlton.

Karlton ignored him. "This is the only chance I've had to dance with her all evening. Go find yourself another partner."

"If you don't want me to flatten you on this floor, *you'd* better find another partner," Emmanuel said.

Shari smiled at their foolishness.

Karlton sighed, kissed Shari on the cheek, and relinquished his hold, and then Shari found herself in Emmanuel's arms, pressed against his body as they moved slowly to the languid beat. As the vocalist sang the lyrics, the bittersweet moment left her mind in turmoil. She pressed her face into his jacket.

"I was afraid I'd miss you," Emmanuel said softly against her ear. "Marry me."

She glanced at him angrily, blinking the glassiness from her eyes. "I haven't seen you for weeks. Suddenly I'm to believe you want to spend the rest of your life with me?"

"Not just weeks, baby. Miserable weeks."

Shari closed her eyes briefly. "Marriage wouldn't work. Right now you're feeling guilty and protective. Soon you'll regret that you even asked."

"Don't tell me that I don't love you, because I do. I haven't been able to sleep a single night since you left. My little hideaway isn't any comfort without you. So I'm asking you to marry me."

Shari noticed Clarice and Johanna whispering to each other, even though they were in their husbands' arms, dancing that last dance.

Emmanuel tugged her chin so that she looked directly at him. "I love you, Shari Jarrod, and I want to spend the rest of my life with you. Before you, commitment was impossible because I'd never met a woman I could live with for the rest of my life—who I couldn't live without. It wasn't commitment that was the problem, it was whom I was with. It just took a while for me to realize what love is."

"That's a sad assed proposal," Emmanuel heard a nosey sister say. "You don't think you're going to get away with that sorry excuse for a proposal. You're the last of the bachelors of your generation. Now you propose the way it should be done."

"Go mind your business," Emmanuel said.

"Not today, I'm not. You've left a string of heartbroken sisters to get away so easy."

"Emmanuel popped the question?" he heard asked.

"We're waiting," the sister said as Shari looked on in horror.

A crowd was beginning to gather. Emmanuel sighed, left with no other recourse.

As in the fashion of *The Best Man,* he dropped to one knee and in a chivalrous and gallant manner proposed formally.

"Hey, you better get up from there," someone said and the crowd began to mutter around them.

"Oh, man, he's fallen like a dead tree struck by lightning."

"Go ahead, girlfriend. Grab him while you've got him."

"He put up a good fight, but he lost."

Then the girls went "aaahhh," and the guys made gagging noises until they were nudged by girlfriends and shushed by parents.

From Emmanuel's mom came, "What's my baby

doing on his knee? My baby!'' and then he heard, ''Mom, please,'' muttered by Johanna.

Nothing was going to be right in his life again. Shari still hadn't responded. She stood indecisive as if she didn't believe a word he'd said. He had put himself on the line. He had so much more to loose now than at the bachelor auction where only his reputation was at stake. Now his heart was involved.

The crowd enclosed them in a circle. Shari stood speechless in the center with Emmanuel as the noise engulfed them.

''Is this the last eligible bachelor I see on bended knee proposing to a woman instead of running fast in the opposite direction?'' Shari heard whispered.

''Let me see what's going on,'' Mrs. Drucilla commanded, and the sea of bodies parted for her. Luke stood at her side. Johanna, Clarice, and Pam beamed beside their husbands with satisfied smiles as if this were all their doing.

''Well, it's about time,'' Mrs. Drucilla pronounced. ''You going to leave him down there all day, Missy?'' she said in her no-nonsense manner.

Shari glanced at Emmanuel again who still held her hand in his. ''Yes,'' she whispered, ''I'll marry you.''

Emmanuel stood, took his bows, and then he kissed her. The crowd erupted in a deafening roar and sang their own rendition of ''You and I.''

ABOUT THE AUTHOR

Reared in Stony Creek, Virginia, best-selling author Candice Poarch portrays a sense of community and mutual support in her novels. She firmly believes that everyday life in small-town America has its own rich rewards.

Candice currently lives in Springfield, Virginia, with her husband and three children. A former computer systems manager, she has made writing her full-time career. She is a graduate of Virginia State University and holds a Bachelor of Science degree in physics.

Dear Readers:

Welcome back to Nottoway. I hope you enjoyed your visit with Emmanuel and Shari. In previous novels, Emmanuel has been the playboy, but now he thought it was time he settled down. At the same time, the triplets are driving him crazy. Karlton has now replaced Emmanuel's playboy image—only to a point. He's in love with Monica. Sounds like a story in the making.

Mrs. Drucilla is getting older now, and she wanted to share her recipe for corn pudding with you. Corn pudding was one of my favorite desserts as a child. I hope you enjoy the recipe as much as the children in Nottoway do.

My next novel, BARGAIN OF THE HEART, set in the Blue Ridge Mountains, will be released in June 2002.

Thank you for so many kind and uplifting letters and for your support.

I love hearing from readers. You may write to me at:

P.O. Box 291
Springfield, VA 22150

With warm regards,
Candice Poarch

MRS. DRUCILLA'S CORN PUDDING

1 15 oz can of corn, drained
5 eggs
2 tbsp flour
1 stick butter or margarine
1½ cups sugar
1 12 oz can evaporated milk (can be fat free)
1 tsp vanilla flavoring
1 box instant vanilla pudding

   Preheat oven to 350 degrees. Lightly grease an eight-inch ovenproof square dish with butter. Mix everything together except the corn and beat. Add corn and mix thoroughly. Pour into the greased dish and place in oven. Let cook until slightly brown on top (approximately 30 to 45 minutes). ENJOY!